Kate Hardy lives in Norwich, in the east of England, with her husband, two young children, one bouncy spaniel, and too many books to count! When she's not busy writing romance or researching local history, she helps out at her children's schools. She also loves cooking—spot the recipes sneaked into her books! (They're also on her website, along with extracts and stories behind the books.) Writing for Mills & Boon has been a dream come true for Kate—something she wanted to do ever since she was twelve. She's been writing Medical Romances™ for Mills & Boon for over ten years now. She says it's the best of both worlds, because she gets to learn lots of new things when she's researching the background to a book: add a touch of passion, drama and danger, a new gorgeous hero every time, and it's the perfect job!

Kate's always delighted to hear from readers, so do drop in to her website at: www.katehardy.com

DR CINDERELLA'S MIDNIGHT FLING

BY
KATE HARDY

First published in Great Britain 2012
by Mills & Boon, an imprint of Harlequin (UK) Limited.
Large Print edition 2012
Harlequin (UK) Limited, Eton House,
18-24 Paradise Road, Richmond, Surrey TW9 1SR

© Pamela Brooks 2012

ISBN: 978 0 263 22471 9

Harlequin (UK) policy is to use papers that are natural, renewable and recyclable products and made from wood grown in sustainable forests. The logging and manufacturing process conform to the legal environmental regulations of the country of origin.

Printed and bound in Great Britain
by CPI Antony Rowe, Chippenham, Wiltshire

Praise for Kate Hardy

'When you pick up a romance novel
by Kate Hardy, you know that you're going to be
reading a spellbinding novel which you will
want to devour in a single sitting,
and A CHRISTMAS KNIGHT
is certainly no exception.'
—*cataromance.com*

'NEUROSURGEON…AND MUM!
is a spellbinding tearjerker readers will
want to read again and again. Written with
plenty of sensitivity, understanding
and heart, NEUROSURGEON…AND MUM! is
the latest winner by this outstanding storyteller!'
—*cataromance.com*

'A wonderfully poignant tale of second chances.
Readers follow the two characters in their quest
for family and everlasting love.
This excellent romance will touch your heart
and have you shedding tears.
ITALIAN DOCTOR, NO STRINGS ATTACHED'
—*RT Book Reviews* 4 Stars

'SURRENDER TO THE PLAYBOY SHEIKH:
I spent a lovely morning with this book,
and I'd advise you to do likewise. Get it.
You'll love it. An unrestrained Grade A.'
—*goodbadandunread.com*

For Fiona—my very best friend and the sister
I wish I had—with much love.

CHAPTER ONE

'CINDERELLA, you are *so* going to the ball,' Sorcha said as Jane opened her front door.

Jane stared at her best friend. 'But I've only just got in from late shift.'

'Perfect timing, then.' Sorcha glanced at her watch. 'The taxi's going to be here in thirty minutes, so you don't have time to argue.'

'I don't have anything to wear.'

'Yes, you do. Right here. It's an unbirthday present from me because I saw it when I was in town and thought the colour was just perfect for you.' Sorcha waved a carrier bag at her. 'Go and have a shower and wash your hair. I'll dry it for you and do your make-up.'

'But—' Jane began, and then subsided. She knew from past experience that, once Sorcha was in full bossy mode, there was no stopping her.

'It's not as if you've got anything better to do

tonight,' Sorcha added. 'And ironing and cleaning your bathroom don't count. You didn't go to a single one of the Christmas nights out, you're always switching your duty so you can avoid team nights out, and it's well past time you stopped letting Shaun ruin your life.'

Jane didn't have an answer for any of that. She knew it was all true.

Sorcha hugged her swiftly. 'I know he hurt you badly, Janey, but you can't hide behind work for the rest of your life. Look, I'm not telling you to go and have a wild fling with the first man you meet. Just come out with me tonight and enjoy yourself. Have some fun.'

Jane wrinkled her nose. 'There's a teensy problem. I don't actually have a ticket for the ball.' She'd given a donation toward the funds instead.

'Actually, you do have one. From Maddie and Theo, with their love—and she says if you say you can't accept it, then she'll accept a promise of babysitting one evening in return, but you're coming to the ball and that's final. And Theo echoed the lot.'

Jane knew when she was beaten. 'I can hardly argue with my boss,' she said wryly.

'Attagirl.' Sorcha smiled at her. 'You've got twenty-seven minutes. Go, go, go!'

By the time the taxi arrived, Jane hardly recognised herself. She normally kept her hair tied back in a ponytail at work, but Sorcha had blow-dried it into a sleek bob. Her make-up was light but still managed to emphasise her hazel eyes and make them sparkle. And the dress was the prettiest she'd ever seen, with a swishy skirt that made her feel light on her feet; it fitted as if it had been made to measure.

'Perfect,' Sorcha said with an approving nod. 'Let's go.'

'What do you mean, you can't make it?' Ed asked.

'I'm stuck in Suffolk,' George explained.

Ed's heart skipped a beat as a nasty thought hit him. 'Is Dad all right?'

'As far as I know. I'm not at the hall.'

'Uh-huh.' So there could only be one other reason why his older brother was standing him up,

Ed thought. He'd had a better offer than a hospital charity ball. 'A girl,' he said with a sigh.

'No, actually. My car had a slight argument with a tree.'

'*What*? Are you all right?'

'I'm fine. Nobody's hurt, except the car. Stop fussing,' George said. 'Metal's easily fixed.'

'I'm a doctor. If you tell me you've crashed your car, of course I'm going to fuss,' Ed retorted.

'Honestly, I'm fine. Not a scratch on me—unlike my poor car. I'll be back in London later in the week. I'm just sorry I've let you down.'

'Just as long as you're really OK. What happened?'

'I took the corner a bit too fast,' George said cheerfully. 'But I've learned my lesson, so don't nag. I spent *hours* polishing that chrome to perfection. I'll be more careful in future.'

Ed could see exactly why his stepmother had begged him to talk some sense into his older brother. Not that he thought George would actually listen to him, but maybe some of Ed's seriousness and common sense would rub off on George and he'd steady down a bit. 'OK.

I'll see you when you're back. Try not to break your neck.'

George just laughed. 'Have a good time tonight.'

Ed replaced the receiver and straightened his bow tie. Well, it wasn't the end of the world that he had to go to the ball on his own. It was a chance to meet some of his new colleagues and have some fun, as well as raising money for specialist equipment at the London Victoria.

He'd liked Theo Petrakis, the senior consultant, at their first meeting. And the photograph of the three little girls on his desk had sealed the deal: Theo was very clearly a family man. Just as Ed was, too; his decision to move back to London from Glasgow was less to do with being promoted and more to do with being nearer to his brother and his sisters. Prompted partly by a quiet phone call from Frances saying that George desperately needed someone to talk sense into him before he broke his neck doing some extreme sport or other.

That was Ed's slot in the family: the younger son of Lord Somers was the sensible, serious one who fixed things. George, the heir to the barony, dated a different gorgeous girl each week and would be the first one down a double black diamond ski run, making him a firm favourite with the paparazzi. And sometimes Ed really worried that his brother was going too far. Still. There was nothing he could do about it tonight. Once George was back in London, he'd take his brother out to dinner and see if he could talk him into calming down just enough to stop the rest of the family worrying themselves sick about him.

'Jake's over there—and he's on his own,' Jane pointed out as she and Sorcha walked into the ballroom.

'And?'

'Sorcha, this is the *ball*. It's your chance to get him to notice that you're stunning as well as good at your job.'

Sorcha shrugged. 'Some other time. I'm not abandoning you on your first night out since...' Her words tailed off.

Jane met it head on. 'Since Shaun.' Her ex-fiancé. Who'd cheated on Jane with her twin sister and shattered every illusion Jane had. 'I know. But it's not as if I don't know most of the people here. I can look after myself.' Jane smiled at her. 'And anyway, I need to find Maddie and Theo to thank them for the ticket. Go and talk to Jake.'

'Are you sure?'

'Very sure.' Jake and Sorcha would make a great couple; Jane thought he just needed to wake up and see what was right under his nose. 'Go for it. I'll see you later. Good luck!'

Once Sorcha was on her way over to Jake, Jane sought out her boss and his wife. 'Thank you so much for the ticket.'

'Our pleasure, Janey,' Maddie Petrakis said, hugging her. 'I'm just glad Sorcha talked you into it.'

'But I'm definitely babysitting for you. Two nights,' Jane added.

'Janey, you look lovely.' Theo, the senior consultant on the maternity ward, gave her an appreciative smile. 'If I was single, I'd be sweeping you off your feet.'

'Yeah, yeah.' She flapped a dismissive hand.

Everyone knew that Theo only had eyes for his wife. But the compliment still pleased her.

'I love your shoes,' Maddie said. 'And have you had your hair done? It's gorgeous.'

'Sorcha nagged me into letting her blow-dry it,' Jane confessed.

'Good for her. Keep it like that,' Maddie said. 'Even if it means getting up twenty minutes early. Because it really suits you.'

Again, the compliment warmed Jane. Maddie was one of her favourite colleagues, and had been a real rock when the hospital grapevine had been buzzing about her last year. Having been through a similar thing with her first husband, Maddie understood exactly how Jane felt about Shaun's very public betrayal. And she'd joined with Sorcha in helping Jane keep her head held high and ignoring the gossip.

'Have you bought your tombola tickets yet?' Maddie asked. 'The prizes are brilliant this year.'

'If there's a balloon ride among the prizes, Dr

Petrakis,' Theo said, 'then we're buying every single ticket until we get it.'

Maddie actually blushed, and Jane laughed. 'I won't ask you what *that's* about. But, yes, I'll buy tickets. And I'll do a stint selling them, if you want.'

'No backstage stuff for you, Dr Cooper. You're here to dance your feet off,' Maddie said. 'Tonight's all about having fun.'

'And raising money for hospital equipment.'

'That, too. OK, you can go and buy loads of tombola tickets—and then you get on that dance floor,' Maddie said. 'Actually—that's senior consultant's orders, isn't it, Theo?'

'Certainly is,' Theo agreed with a smile. 'Actually, I'm trying to keep an eye out for our new consultant. He doesn't start officially until next week, but Maddie bullied him into buying a ticket for the ball.'

'I was off duty when he met everyone else in the department,' Jane said. 'What's he like?'

'A nice guy. He'll fit in to the department, no

problems,' Theo said. 'You'll like him. Which is just as well, as he's going to be working with you.'

'So if I don't see him tonight, I'll meet him on Tuesday morning.'

'Yes. Now, go and enjoy yourself,' Maddie ordered with a smile.

Jane had got halfway over to the tombola table when her phone beeped. She looked at the screen automatically—the senior midwife had promised to get in touch if there were any complications with Ellen Baxter, a patient Jane was worried about—but the message wasn't from Iris. It was from her twin, the one person Jane didn't want to hear from tonight. She groaned inwardly. Right now, she was feeling good about herself, and Jenna always managed to change that within the space of ten seconds.

Even the title of the message stung: PJSB. Short for 'Plain Jane, Super-Brain', the nickname Jenna had coined when they were ten and Jane had won a scholarship to the local private school. Jenna had inherited their mother's genes and was tall and beautiful and effortlessly skinny; compared to her, any woman would look plain. But Jenna had always been quick to point out that Jane was six inches shorter than her, plain and dumpy—especially during their teenage years, and Jane's confidence in the way she looked had reached rock bottom. Jenna had spread the hated nickname among the popular girls at school, to the point where Jane had simply retreated into her books to avoid them.

She meant to close the screen without reading the message—she'd learned the hard way that Jenna only ever contacted her when she wanted something, so it could wait until tomorrow—but she accidentally pressed the wrong button and the words came up on the screen.

Soz it came out lik dis. U shda dun da i/view.

Interview? What interview?

Then Jane remembered. Jenna's publicist had wanted her to be interviewed a few months ago for a *Celebrity Life* feature about twins, along the lines of Jenna being the beauty and Jane being the brains. Jane had been in the middle of exams and simply hadn't had time to do an interview, much less spend a day on a photo shoot. She'd explained why, and thought that was an end to it—but clearly they'd gone ahead with the idea anyway.

Even though she knew it was a bad move, she couldn't help clicking on the attachment.

And then she really wished she hadn't done it. She definitely hadn't posed for that photograph. It looked as if it had been taken after she'd been at the tail end of a busy week on night shifts. She was wearing ratty sweat pants and an old T-shirt under a zipped hooded jacket that had seen better days, with her hair tucked under a woolly hat— clearly ready to do her daily run before crashing into bed. There was nothing in the article about what Jane actually did for a living; it was all about Jenna and unidentical twins.

Worse still, the magazine was going to be on sale in the hospital shop, where everyone could see it. She'd better warn Theo, because it wasn't going to look good for the department. But not right now; it wasn't often that he and Maddie had a night out, and Jane didn't want to spoil things for them. There wasn't anything anyone could do about it right now in any case, so leaving it until tomorrow was the right thing to do.

She closed the phone, but the question buzzed round her head. Why did Jenna hate her so much? Jane had tried and tried and tried to be supportive to her twin. She knew it wasn't easy, being a supermodel. You were always in the public eye; you had to watch what you did and said and ate and drank, and whatever you did people would twist it to suit their own ends. Plus there were always new models coming along, ready to take your place in the spotlight. Not to mention those who were quick to take advantage. It was a lonely, precarious business that had left their mother fragile and prone to bouts of serious depression. Jenna, too, suffered from headaches and what she called 'nerves', whereas Jane had the constitution of an ox and hardly ever caught so much as a cold. But she'd tried to be kind. She'd looked after them both. She'd never complained, never said or done anything to make them feel they were a burden to her.

And yet nothing she did could ever please Jenna or Sophia. They seemed to resent her and look down on her in equal measure, and Jane had no idea how to change that.

She blew out a breath. Sorcha had talked her into coming to the hospital ball and Jane wasn't going to let her twin get to her tonight. All the same, instead of going to the tombola table, she went to the bar and drank a glass of champagne straight down before ordering a second. The bubbles, to her relief, hit immediately. They didn't take the magazine picture out of her head, but they did at least dull the edge of her misery.

She'd just bought her second glass of champagne and was turning back to the dance floor to go and find someone she knew to chat to and dance with when someone jogged her arm and the entire glassful went over the arm of the man standing next to her, soaking his white tuxedo.

'Oh, no! I'm *so* sorry,' she said, horrified. 'Please excuse me.'

'It was an accident. It's not a problem.' He took a handkerchief from his pocket and mopped up the spill.

The handkerchief wasn't enough; she knew the

champagne was going to leave a stain over his sleeve.

'Please, send me the cleaning bill.' She was about to grab a pen and pad from her handbag to scribble down her details for him when she realised: she didn't have either. The dinky little bag she'd brought tonight was less than an eighth of the size of the bag she normally used—the one that Sorcha always teased her was big enough to carry the kitchen sink as well as everything else. In this one, Jane could just about cram her door key, her wallet and her mobile phone into, and even that was pushing it. She was about to pull out her phone and offer to text him her details when he smiled.

'It's fine,' he said. 'Really. But if you want to make amends, you could dance with me.'

She blinked. What? The guy looked like James Bond. Dark hair, piercing blue eyes, and a smile that made her feel as if her temperature had just gone up six degrees. He was the kind of man that attracted third glances, let alone second. 'Dance with you?' she asked stupidly.

He shrugged. 'It's what people are supposed to do at a charity ball, isn't it?'

'I…' Yes. But this man was a stranger. The epitome of a tall, dark, handsome stranger. 'Well, if you're sure. I'm J—'

'No names,' he cut in, smiling to take the sting from his words. 'I rather like the idea of dancing with a gorgeous stranger. Cinderella.'

Gorgeous? Even Sorcha's skill with make-up couldn't make her look as stunning as her mother and her sister. Jane knew she was just ordinary. All the same, she smiled. 'If I'm Cinderella, does that make you Prince Charming?'

'Are you looking for a Prince Charming?'

'No. I don't need rescuing,' she said. Though it wasn't strictly true. Right now, she could really do with dancing with the best-looking man in the room. To take the sharpness of that article away. Honestly compelled her to add, 'Besides, your toes might really regret that offer later. I have two left feet.'

'I don't. So dance with me anyway,' he said, his eyes crinkling at the corners.

'If you have bruised toes tomorrow, don't say I didn't warn you,' she said.

He laughed. 'Somehow, I think my toes will be just fine.'

And then Jane discovered that Prince Charming could dance. *Really* dance. Moving round the floor with him was like floating. Effortless. He was guiding her, so her footwork couldn't possibly go wrong. She'd never, ever danced like this before, and it was a revelation. This was what it was like not to be clumsy.

When the music changed to a slower number, he didn't let her go. It felt completely natural to move closer. To dance cheek to cheek with him.

His skin was soft against hers, with no hint of stubble—clearly he'd shaved just before coming out tonight—and she could smell the citrus tang of his aftershave. She closed her eyes, giving herself up to the moment. Right now she really could imagine herself as Cinderella, dancing with her Prince Charming as he spun her round the floor.

And then she felt him move slightly. His lips brushed against the corner of her mouth.

If she pulled away, she knew he'd stop. All her

instincts told her that her gorgeous stranger was a gentleman.

But what if she moved closer? Would he kiss her properly?

Even the idea of it made her pulse rate speed up and her breathing become shallower.

And then she did it. Moved just a little bit closer.

His arms tightened round hers, and his mouth brushed against hers. Sweet, tempting, promising: and it sent a shiver all the way through her. It had been way too long since she'd been kissed; she couldn't help responding, tipping her head back just the tiniest bit to give him better access to her mouth.

She kept her eyes closed, concentrating purely on the touch of his lips against hers. The way it made her skin feel super-sensitised; the way he coaxed her into responding, kissing him back. Tiny, sweet, nibbling kisses, almost like a dance in itself, leading each other further and further on.

She couldn't help opening her mouth, letting him deepen the kiss. And either that glass of champagne had seriously gone to her head, or

Prince-Charming-meets-James-Bond was the most amazing kisser she'd ever met, because he made her feel as if she were floating. As if there was nobody else in the room, just the two of them and the music.

He kissed her through the rest of the song. And maybe the next, too, because when he broke the kiss she realised that it was a fast dance, and they were swaying together, locked in each other's arms as if it were still a slow dance, even though the band was playing something uptempo.

He blinked then, as if he were just as shocked.

'Wow. It's been a long time since someone's had that effect on me, Cinders,' he said softly.

'You're telling me.' She couldn't remember re-acting like this to anyone, ever. Even to the man she'd once planned to marry.

He leaned forward and stole a kiss. 'Let's get out of here.'

Leave a ballroom where she knew most of the people there, to go to some unspecified place with a complete stranger she'd only just met and whose name she didn't even know? She'd have to be crazy.

Or very, very angry and hurt. Enough to think that going off with the most gorgeous-looking man she'd ever seen—a man who'd kissed her to the point where she'd forgotten where she was—would make her feel much, much better.

'What did you have in mind?' she asked.

'I have a room here,' he said. 'So I was thinking room service. More champagne. Freshly squeezed orange juice. And a toasted cheese sandwich.'

If he'd said caviar or lobster, she would've said no. But the homeliness of a toasted cheese sandwich… Now that was seriously tempting. 'Yes. On condition.'

'Condition?'

'No names. No questions.'

His eyes widened. 'Just one night? Is that what you're saying?'

'Yes.' Tomorrow morning she'd be back to being Plain Jane, Super-Brain. Well, not quite, because she was off duty and she'd actually be Plain Jane who needed to catch up with cleaning her flat. But he'd just made her feel beautiful. Cherished. And she wasn't quite ready to let that feeling go. 'One night.'

'Allow me one question. You're not involved with anyone?'

That was an easy one to answer. 'No.' Though she appreciated the fact that he'd asked, because she needed to know the same thing. The fact that he'd asked first made it easy for her. 'Are you?'

'No.' He caught her lower lip briefly between his. 'Then let's go.'

She walked with him into the hotel reception; while he collected his key, she texted Sorcha. *Bit of a headache, having an early night. Enjoy the rest of the ball, J xx*

It wasn't that far from the truth. She was having an early night. Just…not at home. And the headache excuse was enough to make sure that Sorcha didn't ring the flat to see how she was and worry when there was no answer.

'Everything all right?' Prince Charming asked.

'Fine.' She smiled back at him. 'Just texting my best friend to say I'm leaving, so she doesn't worry that I've disappeared.'

'Which means you're all mine. Good.'

CHAPTER TWO

ED USHERED his Cinderella over to the lifts. Her face was incredibly expressive; as the doors closed behind them, he could see that she was starting to have second thoughts. And third.

She was definitely the responsible, thoughtful type, because she'd made sure that her best friend wasn't worrying about her rather than disappearing without a word. And she was clearly wondering whether she was doing the right thing now.

He took her hand, pressed a reassuring kiss into her palm and curled her fingers over the imprint of his lips. 'Stop worrying,' he said softly. 'You can say no and it won't be a problem. Just come and have a drink with me.'

'I don't normally do this sort of thing,' she muttered, and more colour flooded into her face.

'Me, neither,' he said. 'How shockingly bold of us.'

To his relief, she responded to the teasing note in his voice and smiled back. 'I guess so.' And she made no protest when he unlocked his room and gestured for her to go inside.

'Take a seat,' he said. Though he wasn't surprised that she pulled the chair out from under the dressing table rather than sitting on the bed. 'Shall I order some champagne?'

She gave him a rueful smile. 'I think I've already had enough. So unless you're planning to drink the whole bottle yourself...' She wrinkled her nose. 'Probably not.'

'You spilled most of your glass over me,' he pointed out.

She winced. 'I know, and I'm sorry.'

He shook his head. 'I didn't mean *that*. I wasn't intending to make you grovel, just pointing out that you haven't had a drink tonight.'

'Actually, I have.' She bit her lip. 'This is going to sound terrible, but I drank one glass straight down before the one I spilled over you.'

Now that did surprise him. She'd looked slightly vulnerable when she'd first met him, but he'd assumed that was simply embarrassment at spilling her champagne over him. 'Why? Didn't you want to come to the party?'

'No, it's not that. The hospital ball's always fun.' She blew out a breath. 'We said no questions, remember.'

He shrugged. 'Fair enough.' Though he still wondered. Why would a woman with such beautiful eyes and such a perfect mouth need to bolster her courage with champagne?

'Why do you have a room here?' she asked.

He smiled. 'And who was it who just reminded me, "no questions"?'

'Sorry.' She bit her lip. 'I'm not much good at this. I never go off with complete strangers whose name I don't even know.'

Neither did he. But then again, he hadn't responded so powerfully to someone for a long time; if he was honest, he hadn't felt like that about his wife. And he'd avoided dating since his marriage had disintegrated.

His sisters were all nagging him to have some fun and start dating again. And the way Cinderella had kissed him back on the dance floor had really stirred his blood. He had the feeling that this was something they *both* needed. Except she was clearly worried about him being a stranger. 'That's an easy one to sort. My name's—' he began.

'No,' she cut in. 'We're at a charity ball for the hospital. So the chances are, if you were a complete snake, you wouldn't be here. Or else someone would've warned me about you beforehand and I'd know to avoid you.'

He blinked. 'The grapevine's that fast?'

'Yup.'

'So you work at the hospital,' he said thoughtfully.

'No questions,' she reminded him.

He smiled. 'It wasn't a question. It was a logical deduction. This is a charity ball for the hospital, and you clearly know people, plus you've been to the ball before and you know how fast the grapevine works. QED.'

'And you had an expensive education.' She smiled at his raised eyebrow. 'Again a logical deduction. Most people don't use Latin abbreviations in everyday speech.'

'So the fact you recognise it says the same about you,' he parried.

'Not necessarily. I might be a crossword addict.'

'I like fencing with you,' he said. 'Almost as much as I like dancing with you.' His gaze held hers. 'And almost as much as I like kissing you.'

Colour bloomed in her face, but this time it wasn't shyness. The way her lips parted slightly and her pupils grew larger told him that she liked remembering the way they'd kissed, too.

He took her hand; this time, instead of kissing her palm, he kissed her wrist right where her pulse was beating madly. The longer his mouth lingered, the more her pulse sped up. Her skin was so soft. And she smelled gorgeous—some floral scent he couldn't quite place, mixed with something else. Soft and sweet and gentle. Irresistible.

'You do things to me, Cinders,' he said softly. 'But I'm not going to push you. Do you mind if I...?' He ran his finger round the collar of his shirt and grimaced.

'Slip into something more comfortable?' she asked, raising an eyebrow.

He laughed. 'Hardly. I just want to feel a bit less—well—formal.'

'Sure.'

'Thank you.' He stood up and removed his jacket, hanging it in the wardrobe. Then he undid his bow tie and the top button of his shirt and let the tie hang loose, and rolled the sleeves of his shirt up.

She sucked in a breath.

'What?' he asked.

'Forget Prince Charming. You're all James Bond,' she said.

He raised an eyebrow. 'Is that a good thing?'

'Oh, yes.' Her voice was husky. 'My best friend and I saw the last film three times at the cinema.'

'Well, just for the record, I hate martinis.'

She smiled. 'So do I.'

'And I don't have a licence to kill.'

She spread her hands. 'The only licence I have is a driving licence.'

He laughed. 'Snap. I like you, Cinderella.' His voice deepened, softened. 'Come here.' It was an invitation, not an order. She paused, clearly weighing it up, then nodded, stood up and crossed the short distance between them.

He cupped her face with both hands. 'A perfect heart shape,' he said softly. 'And right now I really, really want to kiss you. May I?'

'Yes.'

Ed smiled and lowered his mouth to hers. Teasing, enticing, more of those little nibbling kisses that had her twining her fingers through his hair and opening her mouth so he could deepen the kiss.

And, just like it had been between them on the dance floor, he felt desire lance through him.

He pulled away slightly, spun her round and undid the zip of her dress. She arched back as he stroked his way down the bare skin he uncovered. Her skin was so soft; and touching her like this wasn't enough. He wanted more. A hell of a lot more.

Gently, he slid the dress from her shoulders and let it fall to the floor. He drew her back against him, his hands splayed across her midriff and his thumbs stroking the undersides of her breasts through the lace of her bra.

'I want you,' he whispered. 'I want to be with you, skin to skin.'

'Me, too.' The admission was low and throaty, and sent a kick of sheer need through him.

She turned to face him, untucked his shirt from his trousers and undid the rest of the buttons of his shirt. Her hands were gentle and yet sure as she slid her palms across his pecs. 'Nice,' she said appreciatively.

'Thank you.' He inclined his head, acknowledging the compliment. 'I like it when you touch me.'

She smiled back, and pushed the cotton from his shoulders; his shirt pooled on the floor next to her dress. She traced the line of his collarbone with one finger.

Good, but not enough. He needed more. He kissed her again, his mouth teasing and demanding at the same time.

He unsnapped her bra, tossed the lace to the floor and then cupped her breasts properly. 'You're beautiful, Cinders.'

No, I'm not. Her thoughts were written all over her face.

Someone—presumably her ex—had really done a number on her. Just as much as Camilla had made him wary of trusting anyone.

'Whoever he was,' Ed said softly, 'he was an idiot.'

'Who?'

'Whoever put that look in your eyes.'

She shrugged. 'You're wearing too much.'

She'd said 'no questions'. And now he had a pretty good idea why. This was starting to look like rebound sex. For both of them.

But they'd agreed from the start that this was one night only. A night out of time. The new hospital was big enough for their paths never to cross again. And if he could make her feel good about herself again tonight, the way she was making him feel good about himself, then that would be a bonus for both of them.

He took her hands and drew them down to his belt. 'Since you think I'm wearing too much, why don't you even things up?' he invited.

Her hands were shaking slightly as she undid

his belt, then the button of his formal trousers, and slid the zipper down.

'You are beautiful, you know,' he said softly. 'Your eyes—I'm not sure if they're green or grey or brown. The colour keeps shifting, and it makes me want to know what colour they are when you're really aroused. And your mouth.' He traced her lower lip with one fingertip. 'It's a perfect cupid's bow. It makes me want to kiss you until we're both dizzy. And here…' He dipped his head and took one hardened nipple into his mouth.

She gave a sharp intake of breath and tipped her head back in pleasure.

Part of Jane knew that this was a seriously bad idea. He was a stranger. And she'd never had a one-night stand before.

Then again, this wasn't a relationship. She didn't have to take the risk of trusting him and then discovering that he had feet of clay, the way she had with Shaun. In a weird kind of way, this was safe—because this man wasn't going to get close enough to her heart to break it.

His mouth teased her lower lip, demanding and getting a response. Jane wasn't sure which of them finished undressing whom, but then he'd lifted her and was carrying her to the bed. She felt the bed dip with his weight, and then the mattress shifted again as he climbed off. She opened her eyes.

'Condom,' he said in answer to her unspoken question.

At least one of them was being sensible. It hadn't even occurred to her. How reckless and stupid was that?

He rummaged in his trousers for his wallet, took out the foil wrapper and placed it on the bedside table.

'You look worried.' He stroked her face. 'If you've changed your mind, I'll understand. I've never forced a woman, and I don't intend to start now.'

'I just...' She hadn't even dated anyone since Shaun's betrayal, let alone slept with anyone. She'd turned down the couple of offers she'd had, not wanting to risk the same thing happening all over again. 'I'm not used to this kind of thing,' she admitted.

'Then let's get used to it together.' He bent his head to kiss her again; his mouth was gentle and promising, rather than demanding. Until she responded, when suddenly the kiss turned hot, turning her into a mass of sheer aching need.

This time, when he touched her, the shyness was gone. She gave herself up to the sensation as he stroked her, teased her, let her touch him in return.

His hand slid between her thighs and she gasped in pleasure.

It really shouldn't be this good for a first time. They didn't even know each other's names, for pity's sake. But it felt as if Prince Charming knew exactly where she liked being touched, exactly how to make her respond to him.

She was near to babbling when she heard the rip of the foil packet and the snap as he rolled on the condom to protect her. Then he eased, oh, so slowly into her. And it was heaven. This was a man who knew exactly what to do—how to give pleasure, how to take her right to the edge and keep her there until she was practically hyper-ventilating.

And then wave after wave of pleasure surged through her as her climax hit. He held her tightly, and she felt the answering surge of his own body against hers.

Gently, he withdrew. 'I'd better deal with the condom. Excuse me a moment,' he said softly.

Jane pulled the sheet back over her, the pleasure replaced by a rush of awkwardness. What did you do on a one-night stand? Did you stay for the whole night, or did you get dressed and leave straight after having sex? She didn't have a clue. She'd never done this kind of thing before; she'd always hung out with the nerdy students, not the wild ones.

He reappeared from the bathroom—still naked, and looking completely unembarrassed about the situation. Clearly he had some idea of the rules; whereas she felt totally at sea.

He climbed into bed beside her and drew her against him. 'What's wrong?'

She sighed. 'If you really want to know, I don't

have a clue what the rules are. What you're supposed to do next on a one-night stand.'

'Once you've had sex, you mean?' He stroked
her hair. 'I don't think there are any rules. What
we do next is entirely up to you.' He smiled.
'Though my vote would be for you to stay a bit
longer and for us to order something from room
service.'

'Your toasted cheese sandwich?'

He shrugged. 'Or whatever you like from the
menu.'

Funny how something so homely could make
her feel so much more at ease. 'Toasted sandwiches would be lovely, thank you. And orange juice.' She smiled at him. 'And can I be
really greedy and ask for coffee as well?' The
champagne she'd gulped down was still fizzing
through her and she really didn't want to spend
the next day with a hangover. OK, so she was a
lightweight, hardly ever drinking more than a
single glass of wine; but she didn't need alcohol
to have a good time.

He smiled back at her. 'Coffee sounds great
to me.'

'And of course I'll pay my half,' she added.

He shook his head. 'My room, my idea and my bill. Don't argue.'

There wasn't much she could say to that, unless she offered to treat him some other night. Which would definitely be breaking the rules—by definition, a one-night stand was for one night only. 'Then thank you,' she said.

'You know,' he said, 'when I came out tonight, didn't think I was going to end up sitting in bed with a perfect stranger, eating comfort food. But I'm really glad I met you, Cinders.'

'Me, too,' she said softly, meaning it.

The sandwiches, when they arrived, were gorgeous. The orange juice was freshly squeezed. And the coffee was among the best she'd ever tasted.

'That was fabulous. Thank you,' she said when they'd finished.

'My pleasure.'

He really was gorgeous. Those piercing blue eyes made her heart skip a beat.

But she didn't want to overstay her welcome. 'And I guess this is my cue to leave.'

'If that's what you really want.' He stole a kiss. 'Or you could…' He paused. 'Stay. Tonight.'

The heat was back in his expression. How could she resist? 'Yes.'

CHAPTER THREE

THE next morning, Jane woke with a start. She was in an unfamiliar bed, in an unfamiliar room, with a body curled protectively round hers.

For a moment she thought she was having some peculiarly vivid dream, remembering what it was like being part of a couple and waking up in her man's arms. But then the body next to hers shifted and pulled her closer.

She was definitely in bed with someone else. And she'd split up with Shaun eight months ago. Which meant that the body curled round hers belonged to… She swallowed hard. She was still in bed with the handsome stranger she'd spilled champagne over last night.

Talk about out of the frying pan and into the fire. What a stupid thing to do: spending the night with a complete stranger, without telling anyone where she was. Even if he did have lovely manners and had given her more pleasure in one night than her ex-fiancé had given her in two years, he was still a stranger. Anything could've happened.

Oh, for pity's sake. Dr Jane Cooper was known for being ultra-sensible. She didn't *do* this sort of thing.

Except…she just had.

At least she hadn't told him her name. Hopefully their paths wouldn't cross so they could avoid an embarrassing situation. Even if they both worked at the London Victoria, the hospital was big enough for her not to know at least half the staff; and she definitely hadn't met him before, or she would've remembered those beautiful eyes.

She'd needed practically no persuasion to spend the whole night with him. And they'd spent most of the night making love. They'd actually run out of condoms, and she'd felt like the bad girl she'd never actually been.

It wasn't that she had regrets about last night—how could she regret the way he'd made her feel?—but she really didn't have a clue how to face him this morning. What to say. How to deal with the situation. Plus she needed to be somewhere. So the best thing she could do would be to slip quietly away before he woke. It would avoid embarrassment on all sides. Gradually, she worked her way out of his arms; when he moved to pull her back again, she gave him the warm pillow she'd been lying on, and he cuddled that closer.

Cute.

Jane smiled regretfully. Maybe if they'd met under other circumstances... But there was no point dwelling on it, and she really needed to check on a patient and talk to her boss.

She picked up her clothes from the floor and quickly dragged them on, rescued her handbag and her shoes, tiptoed over to the door, and unlocked it very quietly. When she glanced back towards the bed, she could see that he was still sleeping. 'Thank you,' she mouthed silently. 'For making me feel beautiful.'

Then she remembered. His jacket. Considering it had been her fault, the least she could do was pick up the dry cleaning bill.

There was a leather folder on top of the dressing table, with the hotel's crest stamped on it. Just as she'd hoped, it contained paper and a pencil. She slid the top sheet quietly out of the folder and scribbled a quick note on it. Then she took some money from her purse and left it on top of the note, then put the pencil on top of the banknotes to weigh them down. Finally, she closed the door behind her and fled.

Back at her flat, Jane showered—trying not to think about what Prince Charming had done with her in his shower last night—and changed into jeans and a plain T-shirt. Once she'd downed a mug of coffee, she flicked into her phone and read the article again, just to be sure that she wasn't making a fuss over nothing.

She wasn't.

She sighed and closed her eyes briefly. There was no point in trying to call Jenna to task over it. Her twin would simply open her big brown eyes and claim innocence, say it wasn't *her* fault the journalist had written it that way. And then somehow their mother would get wind of the row and she'd have a panic attack; and the blame for that would be laid firmly at Jane's door. Been there, done that, worn the T-shirt until it was in rags.

So instead of asking Jenna what her problem was and why she couldn't play nicely for once, Jane sent her a very polite email, saying simply, *Thank you for letting me know.* Even Jenna couldn't twist that.

And now she was going to have to do some damage limitation, as well as check up on how Ellen Baxter was doing this morning.

'You're supposed to be off duty, Jane,' Iris, the senior midwife, said as Jane walked into the department.

Jane smiled. 'I know. Thanks for sending that message through Theo last night.'

'Did you have a good time at the ball?'

'Yes, thanks.'

'Are you sure?' Iris gave her a concerned look. 'You're looking a bit…well, worried, this morning.'

'You know me. Always worrying about my patients,' Jane said lightly. She knew Iris would be sympathetic if she told the midwife about that horrible article, but she needed to tell Theo first. And if anyone was too nice to her right now, she might just bawl her eyes out—from frustration as much as hurt. 'Talking of patients, I'm just going to see Ellen.'

Ellen Baxter was listlessly flicking through a magazine, but she brightened when Jane walked into her room. 'Dr Cooper!'

'Good morning, Ellen.' Jane's smile was genuine. 'How are you doing?'

'OK. I hope.' Ellen grimaced. 'I'm trying to relax.'

'But it's hard when you're on bed rest and you want to be at home.' Jane patted her hand sympathetically. 'Let me have a look at your charts.' She read through them swiftly. 'OK. Can I check your blood pressure and your temperature?'

'You can stick as many needles as you like in me, if it means I can go home!' Ellen said.

Jane laughed. 'You're safe from needles today.' She checked Ellen's blood pressure and temperature, then marked them on the chart. 'That's good. Any twinges or spotting?'

'None. And, believe you me, I'd say if there

was,' Ellen said feelingly. 'I don't want anything to go wrong. I can't lose this baby.'

'I know,' Jane soothed. 'We're all rooting for you.'

'Everyone's being so nice here, but it's just not home.' Ellen flushed. 'And I know it's wet of me, but I can't sleep properly without Rob.'

'It's not wet. It's perfectly understandable.' It had taken Jane weeks to get used to sleeping on her own after she'd split up with Shaun. Luckily she'd been the one to move, so at least there were no memories of him in her flat. 'Ellen, I'm happy with your obs. If Rob can come and pick you up, then I'll discharge you this morning. With conditions,' she added firmly.

'Anything,' Ellen said, her eyes shining.

'Firstly, you take it easy. Secondly, any worries at all—no matter how small or how silly you think they might be—you call me. Thirdly, any twinges, you get straight here to the department. OK?'

'OK.' Ellen's eyes filled with tears. 'You've been so lovely. If it wasn't for you...' Her voice cracked.

Jane squeezed her hand again. 'That's what I'm here for.' She smiled at Ellen and got off the bed. 'You call Rob, and I'll get the paperwork sorted with Iris.'

'Thank you. Thank you so much.' Ellen's eyes glittered with tears.

Warm and soft in his arms… Ed snuggled closer, then realised drowsily that he wasn't holding someone, he was holding some*thing*. He opened his eyes. A pillow.

She'd left him asleep, holding a pillow.

Unless maybe she was in the shower? He listened, but he could hear nothing from the bathroom. And the sheet on her side of the bed was stone cold. She'd been gone for a while.

Well, he supposed it was one way to avoid the awkwardness. Though it stung that she hadn't waited for him to wake up.

On his way to the bathroom, he saw the note on the dressing table.

Dear Prince Charming, Thank you for last night. Hope this covers the dry cleaning bill. Cinders.

So she'd played the game right to the end. He damped down the surge of disappointment that she hadn't left him her number or told him her real name.

And there was the fact that she'd left him some money. He knew she'd meant it to cover the cleaning bill for his jacket, but it still made him feel cheap.

Still, it was his own fault for acting on impulse. He was better off being his usual sensible, serious self. And he wouldn't make that mistake again.

Once the paperwork was done, it was time to start the damage limitation. Jane knocked on Theo's open office door.

He looked up from his desk. 'Janey, you're supposed to be off duty. What are you doing here?' He raised one hand to silence her reply. 'Oh, don't tell me. Ellen Baxter.'

'Yes. I'm discharging her this morning. She'll call me if she has any worries and she'll come straight back here if she has the slightest twinge.'

'And did you come in to tell me that, or to bring me coffee?' he asked, looking hopeful.

'Actually, a large brandy might be more in order,' she said ruefully.

He frowned. 'What's up, Janey?'

She dragged in a breath. 'I need to show you something. I'm sorry, I had absolutely no idea about it until I got the email last night.' She pulled the article up on her phone and handed it to him.

Theo read through it, his mouth set in a grim line; when he'd finished, he looked up at her. 'I've never seen such utter spite in my entire life. I can't believe this is focused on something so shallow and it doesn't even say what you do! Are you all right?'

No. She was ragingly angry and desperately hurt. She yanked the emotions back. No more tears. Just smiles. 'I'm fine,' she fibbed. 'But this is going to look really bad for the department. If you want me to resign, I understand.'

'Resign? You must be joking. Janey, you're an excellent doctor and this rubbish has got nothing to do with you.' He flicked out of the screen. 'When does the magazine go on sale?'

'I'm not sure. This week, I think.'

'Right. I'll have a word with the shop manager

and make sure it's not on sale in the hospital this week. If necessary, I'll buy their entire stock of the magazine myself. I can't do anything about people who buy it elsewhere and bring it in, but my guess is that anyone who knows you—staff or patient—will be fuming on your behalf.' He looked grim as he handed the phone back to her. 'And those who choose to spread gossip or make stupid comments to you—well, their opinions are worth nothing in the first place, so just ignore them, OK?'

'Thank you.' She felt humble beyond belief that her boss was prepared to buy up the entire stock of magazines to try and spare her from an awkward situation.

'I take it that—' he said something in Greek that she didn't understand, but from the expression on his face it definitely wasn't anything complimentary '—sister of yours was behind this?'

Jane spread her hands. 'She asked me to do the interview months ago. It was meant to be a feature about twins, "the beauty and the brains". Except I was up to my eyes with work and exams, so I said I couldn't do it. I thought she'd just forgotten about it.'

'More like she used it to have another dig at you, because she's incredibly jealous of you.'

'She can't be. There's absolutely nothing to be jealous about. She's a supermodel,' she reminded Theo.

'She's also heading towards thirty and she's not going to get the same kind of work opportunities she had when she was eighteen. Looks don't last, but education does. You're clever, your career will be going from strength to strength while hers is starting to go more slowly, and everyone who meets you really likes you. *That's* why she's jealous,' Theo said. He sighed. 'Do your parents know about this?'

'Probably not. But I'm not going to say anything. You know my mum's fragile.'

'I know depression's tough to overcome,' Theo said gently, 'but it doesn't mean you can just give up on being a parent to your children. When have either of your parents ever put you first?'

Jane didn't want to answer that. 'It's OK.'

Theo gave her a sympathetic look. 'You've got more patience than anyone else I know.'

'It's not easy for Mum. She was right at the height of her career when she fell pregnant with Jenna and me and had to give it all up.' According to Sophia, pregnancy had ruined her skin and her figure; and, with the crippling post-natal depression she'd suffered afterwards, she'd never been able to return to her modelling.

'You know, Maddie could say the same thing. Being a mum means that she's had to give up some of her career choices, and I've turned down offers as well because I don't want a job that'd mean I can't give her and our daughters enough time. But neither of us would change a thing, because the girls have brought so much joy to us,' Theo said softly.

Jane had to swallow hard. What would it be like to have a family who loved her unconditionally, the way Maddie and Theo felt about their children, instead of making her feel guilty for being born? What would it have been like if Jenna had supported her and cheered her on through the long years of studying medicine, instead of pulling her down and mocking her all the time?

Though it was pointless dwelling on it. She couldn't change the way they were. All she could do was try to love them as best as she could—and, since Shaun had betrayed her with Jenna, that had meant from a safe distance. Which, she supposed, made her just as bad as them.

Theo reached out and squeezed her hand. 'Sorry. I'm overstepping the mark. It's not my place to criticise your family. Though I wish they'd appreciate you for who you are.'

He paused. 'Do you want me to call Maddie? Or Sorcha?'

'No. I'll be fine.'

'Hmm.' He looked at her. 'Is that article the reason why you disappeared from the ball so early last night?'

'No.' Not exactly. She definitely wasn't telling him the real reason behind that.

'Sure?'

'Sure,' she confirmed.

'I'll believe you—for now.' He smiled at her. 'Now, go and have two nice days off, forget about that stupid article, and come back all bright-eyed on Tuesday morning, yes?'

'OK, Theo.' She dragged in a breath. 'And thank you.'

'Any time.'

On Tuesday morning Jane had just checked up on her first patient when Theo walked in. 'Janey, have you got a moment?'

She looked over at him, saw the man in the white coat next to him, and her knees went weak as she recognised him.

Oh, my God.

He couldn't possibly be… Could he?

Theo's next words confirmed it. 'I'd like to introduce you to our new consultant.'

If Theo said his name was James or Bond, she was going to collapse in a puddle of hysterical laughter.

'Edward Somers,' Theo continued. 'Ed, this is Jane Cooper, one of our F2 doctors, but it's not going to be long before she makes registrar.'

She could feel her face going bright red and there was a tiny, tiny smile lifting the corner of

Ed's mouth. Oh, please, don't let him say anything about Saturday night…

'Good to meet you, Jane,' he said politely.

Then she realised she'd been holding her breath, waiting for him to spill the beans. Clearly he wasn't going to do that: because it wouldn't reflect too well on him, either. She smiled at him in relief. 'You, too, Edward—or do you prefer Ed?'

For a second, she could swear he mouthed 'James Bond', but then he said, 'Ed. May I join you in your rounds?'

'I—well, sure.' She spread her hands. 'You're the senior. I guess you should lead.'

Ed smiled at her. 'Patients are much more important than protocol. You already know them, so I'm happy for you to lead and introduce me while we're there.'

'I'll leave you in Jane's capable hands,' Theo said, and headed back to his office.

'Very capable,' Ed said softly.

Oh, help.

'I, um… Look, we probably need to talk, but for now can we keep this…well, just work?' Jane asked.

'For now,' he agreed.

Before she could take him to the next patient, Iris hurried over. 'We've just had a call from the ED. The mum's twenty-four, she's eleven weeks pregnant and she can't stop being sick. Marina thinks it's hyperemesis.'

'We're on our way,' Jane said.

In the emergency department, she swiftly introduced Ed to Marina Fenton, the specialist registrar.

'I'm pretty sure it's hyperemesis. Poor woman— morning sickness is bad enough,' Marina said. 'I've already done bloods and sent them off for electrolyte levels, blood count and renal.'

'Thanks, Marina—that's great.'

'Mrs Taylor's through here.' She showed them to the cubicle where a young woman was retching miserably into a bowl.

'Mrs Taylor? I'm Jane Cooper and this is Ed Somers. Dr Fenton asked us to come down and see you. Can I get you a drink of water?' Jane asked.

Mrs Taylor shook her head. 'I can't keep anything down.'

'Taking small sips might help you feel a little bit better,' Jane said gently, and stuck her head out of the cubicle for long enough to ask one of the auxiliaries to bring in a glass of water.

'How long have you been feeling like this?' Ed asked.

'About a month. I knew you got morning sickness, I just didn't expect it to be all day and all night and as bad as this.' She retched again. 'Sorry.'

'You don't have to apologise,' Jane said, squeezing her hand.

The auxiliary brought in the water Jane had asked for, and Mrs Taylor managed a small sip. 'Thank you. That's made my mouth feel a bit less disgusting,' she admitted.

'Good. Have you talked to your family doctor or your midwife about your sickness?' Ed asked.

'I didn't want to bother them.' She shook her head. 'My sister had it bad, too. She lost weight and felt lousy all the time for the first bit.'

Jane and Ed exchanged a glance; hyperemesis was known to run in families. But it was also more common in women carrying twins—or, more rarely, it could be caused by something more sinister. They needed to run some tests to rule out the nasties.

'My boss made me come in. I was sick over a client. It was her perfume that set me off—it was so strong.' Mrs Taylor bit her lip. 'I really hope he forgives me.'

'I'm sure he will. He sent you in because he was worried about you,' Ed reassured her. 'So, you're about eleven weeks. Have you had a scan yet?'

'No, that was meant to be next week. My Jason's getting the day off to come with me.' Worry skittered across her face. 'Is there something wrong with the baby? Is that why I keep being sick like this?'

'I think you have something called hyperemesis—it's basically really bad morning sickness,' Ed said. 'I've treated mums before who've had the same thing. It's really miserable for you, but you're in the right place and we can do something to help you feel a lot better.'

'Really?' Mrs Taylor looked as if she didn't quite dare believe them.

'Really,' Jane confirmed.

'And it won't harm the baby? Only my nan said she knew someone who took stuff to make them stop being sick and the baby was…' She shuddered. 'I feel like death warmed up, but I'd rather put up with that than risk anything happening to the baby.'

'We won't give you anything that's not safe for the baby,' Ed reassured her. 'Dr Fenton told us she's already done some blood tests, so we need to wait for the results of those. But in the meantime we'd like to give you a scan and see how the baby's doing.'

'Has anyone called your husband, or would you like us to call someone to be with you?' Jane asked.

'Jason's on his way,' Mrs Taylor said.

'That's great. We'll to take you up with us to the maternity unit, then,' Jane said.

'And, because you're quite dehydrated from being sick, I'd like to keep you in for a little while and put you on a drip to replace the fluids you've lost. That'll make you feel a lot better, and we have one or two things that will help you stop being sick but won't affect the baby,' Ed reassured her.

By the time they'd taken Mrs Taylor up to the maternity unit, her husband had arrived. Ed ushered them in to the consulting room with the portable scanner, and Jane noticed that he was careful to make sure that the Taylors couldn't see the screen, in case it was bad news.

'What I'm going to do is to put a bit of gel on your stomach—sorry, it's a bit cold, whereas down in ultrasound it's always warm. All it does is help us get a better picture of the baby,' Jane explained. 'It's not going to hurt you or the baby—I'm sure your midwife's already told you this, but it's all done by sound waves.'

Mrs Taylor retched again, and her husband held the bowl for her; when she'd finished, Jane wiped her face with a damp cloth.

'This baby's going to be an only child,' Mrs Taylor said. 'I'm not going through this again. Ever.'

Jane made a soothing noise and glanced at Ed. Please, don't let it be a molar pregnancy causing the sickness, she thought.

Ed returned her glance; as if he could read her mind, he gave her a reassuring smile and the tiniest nod.

Thank God.

'I'm pleased to say that the baby's doing fine.' Ed turned the screen to show them. 'I did wonder if you might be having twins, because that sometimes makes the sickness much worse; but you're having just one. Here's the heart, beating nicely.' He pointed out the baby's heart. 'Everything's looking just as it should do.' He made some quick measurements. 'And you're eleven and a half weeks.'

Mrs Taylor brushed back a tear. 'The baby's really all right?'

'The baby's absolutely fine,' Ed reassured her.

'Can we have a picture?' Mr Taylor asked.

'Unfortunately, this is a portable scanner, so we can't print anything from it. But when you have your proper scan next week, they'll be able to give you pictures then,' Jane explained.

Ed ran through the treatment plan, explaining what they were going to try and why; Jane found herself chipping in from time to time. It was as if she'd worked with him for years, instead of only half a morning. Whatever the complications caused by their fling on Saturday night, she was definitely going to able to work with this man. He fitted right in to the team, and he treated the mums with respect and dignity. And she liked that. A lot.

'I like your bedside manner,' she said when they'd left the Taylors.

He raised an eyebrow. 'Funny, I find sometimes women run from it.'

Jane felt the colour shoot into her face. 'I didn't mean *that* kind of bedside. I meant how you are with the mums. In my last hospital, I worked with a consultant who was incredibly brusque and treated everyone like idiots, mums and staff alike. He had all the social skills of a piranha, and I swore I'd never become like that myself or be forced to work with anyone like that again.' She gave him a wry smile. 'Though I guess I knew you wouldn't be like that, or Theo would've refused to appoint you.'

He smiled. 'I was teasing you, Jane.'

Her face was burning. 'Sorry. Everyone says

I'm too serious. I'm afraid you drew the short straw and you've got the nerdy one to work with.'

'Nerdy's good,' he said. 'I like clever people. Come on, let's finish our rounds.'

She introduced him to the rest of her patients. When they'd finished, he said, 'I think we need to talk. Probably not where we're likely to be overheard, so do you know a quiet corner somewhere?'

Here it came. Retribution for her acting so madly, so unJanelike, on Saturday. And Sunday. 'Believe it or not, the most private place is probably going to be the hospital canteen; it's noisy and people don't get a chance to eavesdrop.'

'Good. Let's go.'

CHAPTER FOUR

'I'M BUYING,' Jane said, trying not to think of the last time they'd had coffee together. 'Black, no sugar, isn't it?'

'Yes, thanks. You have a good memory.'

'Doctors are supposed to be observant,' she said with a smile. She ordered a black coffee, plus a cappuccino for herself. 'Do you want a muffin with that?' she asked.

'No, I'm fine with just coffee, thanks.'

When she'd paid, she found them a quiet corner. 'Thanks for not bringing up what happened on Saturday in the department.'

He shrugged. 'No problem. But we do need to talk about Sunday.'

'Sunday?' She'd expected him to talk about Saturday and how they needed to set some boundaries. They were colleagues, nothing more, and what happened on Saturday wasn't going to be repeated.

'Sunday,' he confirmed. 'I was kind of expecting to see you when I woke up.'

She stirred her coffee, avoiding looking him in the eye. 'You were still asleep when I woke, so I thought it might be less awkward if I just left quietly.'

'Maybe. But when you wake up and someone's left you money after they spent the night with you, it tends to make you feel a bit like a gigolo.'

She nearly choked on her coffee. 'The money was to cover the cleaning bill for your jacket. I didn't mean it to—oh, help. OK.' She blew out a breath. 'Theo didn't introduce me properly. Dr Jane Cooper. Good with patients, but her social skills need a bit of polishing.'

'Want to know how I see it?' Ed asked softly. 'Dr Jane Cooper, who's charming and warm and kind; and, even more charmingly, clearly doesn't have a clue just how lovely she is.'

It was a far cry from Shaun's damning assessment of her when she'd asked him why he'd cheated on her with Jenna. He'd said that she was twenty pounds too heavy and six inches too short. Jane knew it was ridiculous—she couldn't change her height and she had no intention of tottering around in uncomfortable high heels just to please someone else—but it had knocked her confidence as well as destroying her trust. He'd homed in on exactly the same criticisms that Jenna and her mother had always made about her: everything was about appearances, not what lay beneath. She'd thought Shaun was different, that he'd love her for who she was. How rubbish her judgement had turned out to be.

She frowned. 'Look, I'm not fishing for compliments, Ed. I know who I am and I'm comfortable with that.'

'Which is just how things should be,' Ed said.

This was crazy, Ed thought. He didn't do mad things. He was sensible. But on Saturday night he'd swept Jane off her feet and surprised himself. And he wanted to do it all over again.

According to his sisters, he was too reserved and needed to get a life. If he could swap a bit of his common sense for some of George's recklessness, they'd both be a lot more balanced.

Since the divorce, Ed hadn't even dated. He

hadn't trusted his own judgement. And it looked as if Jane too had an ex who'd hurt her badly and had made her wary of relationships. Which left them…where?

He'd felt that they'd had a real connection on Saturday night. Not just the sex—there was something about Jane. Something that made him want to get to know her better. Something that made his customary reserve feel totally wrong where she was concerned. Something that made him want to take a chance.

He'd seen her work. She was calm, competent and knew how to work as a team. So it wouldn't be that much of a risk…would it?

'Given that I didn't get to see you on Sunday, how about you make amends this evening?' he asked.

She looked surprised. 'How do you mean?'

He shrugged. 'Have dinner with me.' He could see the panic skittering across her face. 'Unless you'd rather go and see a film or something?'

The teeniest twinkle of mischief appeared in her eyes. 'Would that be a James Bond film?'

Just how he'd hoped she'd respond. He grinned.

'If you know where one's showing, sure. Or, if not, we could go and find a DVD—though we'd have to watch it at your place. My hotel room doesn't have a DVD player.'

'You're still staying at the hotel?'

He nodded. 'I do have a flat lined up, but I can't move in until the weekend. So the hotel was really the only choice.'

'Don't you have family or friends you can stay with?' Then she grimaced. 'Sorry. I'm being horribly nosey.'

He spread his hands. 'I don't think our "no questions" rule applies any more—and of course you'd want to know more about a new colleague. I was working in Glasgow, but I came back to London to be near my family.'

She frowned. 'So why are you staying in a hotel rather than with them?'

He smiled. 'I love my family. Dearly. But they'd drive me crazy if I went back to live with them after fourteen years of being away—there'd be questions all the time. Far more questions than you ask,' he added, seeing the colour rise in her cheeks. 'And living with my older brother's a definite no-no.' He'd thought about it, on the grounds that maybe he'd be a steadying influence. But then again, George was too strong a character to be influenced by anyone.

'Because you don't get on with him?' Jane asked.

Ed laughed. 'No. I get on fine with George. It's just that I'd never be able to keep up with him. He tends to burn the candle at both ends.'

'And you disapprove of that?'

'Not disapprove, exactly. I worry about him overdoing things. So I guess I'd drive him crazy, the same way the girls always nag me about working too hard.' He paused. 'What about you?'

'I have my own flat.'

Sidestepping again, he noticed. OK. He'd ask her straight out. 'Do you have family in London?'

'No.'

And he noticed she didn't say where her family was. 'You really don't like talking about personal stuff, do you?' he asked softly.

She spread her hands. 'What do you want to know? I'm twenty-eight, I'm working towards being a specialist registrar and I love my job. My parents used to live in London, but they're retired now and they have a place in Cornwall overlooking the sea.' She paused. 'And that's about it.'

Her body language was definitely telling him to back off. So he changed the subject to something he thought she'd find easier. 'What made you want to be a doctor?'

'I'm a fixer,' she said. 'I like to make things better. So it was the obvious career choice.'

'Me, too,' he admitted. 'Why obstetrics?'

'I was interested in IVF,' she said. 'I loved the idea of being able to give people hope, give them the family they'd dreamed about and longed for. Really making a difference.' Giving them the dream family she'd so wanted herself. She pushed the thought away. 'But then I did my rotation on the maternity ward, and I discovered just how much I like babies. There's absolutely nothing to match seeing those first magical seconds of a newborn taking in the world. Oh, and I'd better warn you in advance—it makes me cry every single time.'

He'd guessed she was soft-hearted. From what

he'd seen of her at work so far, she really cared about her mums.

'But Theo knows I'm interested in IVF and I worked with the specialist team for a while, so my list tends to include more IVF mums. It means I've got the best of both worlds—I get to deliver babies, and I also get to look after mums who need a bit of extra care.' She looked at him. 'What made you choose obstetrics?'

'The same thing, really. I'm the fixer in my family, too. Right from when I was small, I used to bandage the dogs' paws and pretend I was making them better.'

'So you wanted to be a vet?'

'When I was that young, yes.' He laughed. 'Luckily the dogs were very indulgent. They'd let me listen to their heart with my stethoscope and stick a bandage on their paw. I was forced to use them as my patients because George—my older brother—was never still for long enough for me to bandage him.' He turned his coffee cup round in his hands. 'My sister Alice got meningitis when she was two. Luckily she was fine, but we spent a lot of time at the hospital, and I was desperate to make her better and make everyone in the family happy again. That's when I decided that I wanted to be a doctor. I thought about being a children's doctor, but then Frances had Bea. She was this little red-faced squeaky thing—just like Alice was—and everyone was smiling and so happy. And I knew then that was what I wanted to do—bring little red-faced squeaky things into the world and spread all that joy around.'

She laughed. 'Do your sisters know you call them red-faced squeaky things?'

'Yes.' He grinned. 'And I'm not going to tell you what they call me. Or what Charlotte calls me, for that matter.'

'Alice, Bea and Charlotte. You're Edward, and you have a brother George,' she mused. 'So who are the D and F?'

He liked the fact she'd picked that up. 'My father's David, and my stepmum's Frances.'

'Are there an H and an I, too?'

'No. And I really hope the girls aren't planning to make me an uncle to H and I before they've finished their education.'

'They're a lot younger than you, then?'

He nodded. 'I'm six years older than Alice. She's just about to be called to the bar, Bea's training to be an architect and Charlotte—the baby—is in the last year of her degree. She's on course for a First, so she's planning to do a PhD in a really obscure bit of Roman history.'

'So you're all clever.' Jane smiled. 'What does George do? Is he a professor of astrophysics or something?'

'He's—' Ed stopped. How much had Theo told the team about him? Or had Jane worked it out for herself that Ed's older brother was the Hon George Somers, heir to the barony? From what he'd seen of Jane, she was very straightforward and absolutely everything showed in her face, so it would be obvious if she read the gossip rags and knew who George was.

'He works in the family business,' Ed prevaricated.

Jane knew a sidestep when she saw one. Probably because she'd learned to be so skilled in side-stepping herself. Ed didn't want to talk about his brother as much as she didn't want to talk about

Jenna. And yet he'd sounded affectionate when he'd said he worried about his brother. Something didn't quite add up, here. Though it was none of her business and she didn't want to pry—in case he started asking questions back.

She glanced at her watch. 'We need to be getting back to the ward.'

'Of course. So are we having dinner or going to the cinema tonight?'

Help. She'd hoped that getting him to talk about himself would've distracted him enough to make him forget the idea of going out. 'It's really nice of you to ask, but I can't make tonight. Some other time?' Though she was careful not to give an excuse that he could easily topple over, or to suggest anything specific—like an actual date when she could go out with him.

'Sure.'

Back on the ward, they were both kept busy, and the rest of the day shot by.

'See you tomorrow,' Ed said. 'Have a nice evening, whatever you're doing.'

Dinner for one and a pile of textbooks. But she liked it that way. 'You, too,' she said with a smile.

Even so, she couldn't get Edward Somers out of her head all evening, and she caught herself mooning over him when she was supposed to be studying. Which was ridiculous. And she was glad when the phone went and the caller display showed her best friend's number.

'Am I interrupting your studies?' Sorcha asked.

'I was about to take a break anyway,' Jane said.

'Hmm. Just checking on how you're doing.'

Jane knew exactly why Sorcha was calling. Because today was the day that horrible magazine had come out. 'I'm fine. Honestly, I am. Nobody on the ward's mentioned that article, and Theo's gone well above the call of duty and arranged that the hospital shop won't sell the magazine this week.' She bit her lip. 'Actually, I think he bought all the copies.'

'If he hadn't, Maddie and I would've clubbed together and done it,' Sorcha said. 'I'm not going to nag you about Jenna, because I know it's hard for you.'

'Good.'

'But I still think she's incredibly mean to you and you're a saint to put up with it.'

'Do you mean doormat?' Jane asked wryly.

Sorcha sighed. 'No, because you don't do it because you're weak. You do it because you're nice, and I guess family relationships are complicated. Though I'd disown her if she was mine. You know, just because you're related to someone, it doesn't mean you have to like them—or put up with them behaving badly towards you.'

Jane just coughed.

'OK, OK, I'll shut up. So what's your new colleague like?'

The gorgeous stranger I spent the night with on Saturday, and still haven't told you about, Jane thought. My guilty secret. 'Fine.'

'Come on. Deets.'

'There aren't any.'

'Well, is he nice?'

'Yes.'

'Single?'

Yes, but she didn't want to tell Sorcha that. Or that Ed had asked her out to dinner tonight. Because then Sorcha would nag her about letting Shaun's betrayal ruin her life. And Jane already knew her best friend's 'the best revenge is living well' speech by heart. 'It's hardly the first thing you'd ask a new colleague.' She really needed to change the subject, now, before she ended up telling Sorcha more than she intended. 'How's Jake?'

'He's wonderful.'

'Good.' Jane smiled. 'It was about time he noticed you. I'm so glad it's working out.'

'I just wish I had a magic wand and could find someone nice for you,' Sorcha said.

'There's no need, honestly. I'm fine on my own.'

'Really? Because I worry that you're lonely. I think what happened with Shaun last year broke something in you.'

It had. 'I guess I learned my lesson the hard way,' Jane said lightly. 'I'm sticking to friendship from now on. It makes life a lot easier.'

'Not every man's as shallow as Shaun was.'

'I know.' Ed definitely wasn't shallow. But she didn't want to analyse her feelings about him too closely. She'd thought she had a future with Shaun, that with him she'd make the close family she'd always wanted, filled with unconditional love. And she'd been so wrong. What was to say that she wouldn't be wrong about Ed, too? One night was just one night, and she was fine with that. 'I'm fine, Sorcha. Really.' Protesting a little too much, perhaps. But she'd get there.

'Well, you know where I am if you need to talk. Even if it's stupid o'clock in the morning.'

'I know, and thank you. I'm just glad you're my best friend.'

'Me, too. Now, don't study too late.'

'I won't,' Jane promised.

'And I'll see you for lunch tomorrow. Call me if you get held up, OK?'

'Will do. See you tomorrow.'

CHAPTER FIVE

'ED, I'VE got one of my mums on the way in. She's bleeding. And I could do with another view on the situation,' Jane said. 'Would you mind?'

'Sure. Fill me in on the background. Is she one of your IVF mums?'

Jane nodded. 'Pippa Duffield. She had a low-lying placenta at her twenty-week scan.'

'Nearly a third of women do. You know as well as I do, in most cases, it stops being a problem as the uterus develops further,' Ed said. 'I take it you're thinking placenta praevia in Pippa's case?'

Jane nodded. 'She's got more than average risk factor. IVF increases the chances of her placenta growing in the lowest part of the womb and covering the opening of the cervix, plus she's having twins.'

'OK. How many cycles did she have, and how old is she?'

'This was the fourth cycle, and she's thirty-eight.'

'So her age is another risk factor.' He looked grim. 'Let's hope for her sake that it's praevia and not an abruption.'

Jane hoped so, too. An abruption, where the placenta tore away from the uterus, could be life-threatening for both the babies and the mum.

Ed looked thoughtful. 'How far is she?'

'Thirty-two weeks.'

'So we'd be considering delivery at thirty-five weeks anyway. Provided we can get the bleeding under control, if the ultrasound shows it's praevia, I'd like to keep her in the ward on bed rest until delivery, so we can keep an eye on her and monitor the babies,' he said. 'Are you happy with that?'

She spread her hand. 'Hey, you're the consultant. It's your call.'

'She's one of your mums. You asked me for my opinion—I'm not muscling in and giving orders you're not happy about.'

'Thank you. Though, actually, my clinical decision would be the same as yours.'

'Good.' He smiled at her. 'I'm glad we're on the same wavelength. It feels as if I've worked with you for years, not just for a day or so.'

Funny how that warmed her. 'Me, too. And that makes life so much easier for our mums.' She smiled back at him. 'I should warn you, Pippa's desperate for a natural birth—the way she sees it, it'll make up for the fact she couldn't conceive without help.'

'That really depends on the ultrasound,' he said. 'If the placenta's within ten millimetres of her cervix, then it's too much of a risk to go for a normal delivery—both for her and for the babies.'

'Agreed,' Jane said.

Jane had asked one of the porters to meet Pippa's taxi and bring her up to the department in a wheelchair; just as she and Ed were sorting out the consulting room, Joe brought Pippa's wheelchair in.

'Thanks, Joe. I appreciate your help,' Jane said with a smile. 'Pippa, how are you doing?'

'I'm so scared, Jane. I can't lose my babies. Not now. Not after all we've been through. I just *can't*.' Pippa's face was blotchy with tears. 'When

I started bleeding…' She dragged in a breath. 'I'm just so scared.'

'Of course you are. Any mum-to-be would be worried, in your shoes, and you did exactly the right thing by coming straight in,' Jane soothed, giving her a hug. 'But first of all remember that you're thirty-two weeks now, so even if the twins arrived today there's a very good chance of them being absolutely fine. And secondly, there are all sorts of reasons why women start spotting or even having quite a big bleed. Until we've examined you, I can't tell you what's happening, but you're in the best place right now. And the best thing you can do for your babies is to take some big, deep breaths for me.'

She coached Pippa through the breathing until the other woman was calmer. 'Brilliant. That's got your blood pressure back down a bit. Now, I'd like to introduce you to our new consultant, Mr Somers. Ed, this is Pippa Duffield.'

'Oh, my God.' Pippa's eyes widened. 'The bleeding's serious enough for me to see a *consultant*?'

'No. I'm just the new boy, it's my first week

here, and I'm working with Jane,' Ed said cheerfully.

'And he's very good,' Jane said. 'More experienced than I am. So between us you're in great hands.'

Pippa gave her a wan smile.

'May we examine you, Mrs Duffield?' Ed asked.

'Call me Pippa,' she said. 'Yes.'

'Thank you, Pippa. And I hope you'll call me Ed.'

She nodded.

Gently, he examined her. 'Are you feeling any kind of pain?'

'No.'

'Good. Are you having any kind of contractions, even practice ones or tiny ones?'

'I don't think so.'

He nodded. 'Jane, would you mind checking the babies' heartbeats?'

Jane did so. 'The good news here is that their heartbeats both sound normal. Now, at this stage, we're not going to do an internal exam, Pippa.' Until they were sure it was placenta praevia and not an abruption, she didn't want to take the risk of causing a much worse bleed. 'But we'd like to do an ultrasound so we can get a better idea of what's causing the bleeding, if that's OK with you, Pippa?'

'The babies are all right. Thank God.' Pippa closed her eyes briefly in seeming relief. 'Do whatever you need to, Jane.'

'I'll also need to take some blood,' Jane said.

She swiftly took blood samples and assessed how much blood Jane had lost, before putting a line in for IV access; meanwhile, Ed had gone to locate the portable ultrasound scanner.

The scan showed exactly what she and Ed had expected.

'Your placenta's right near the bottom of your womb and it's partially blocking your cervix,' Ed said. 'What happens in the last trimester of pregnancy is that your cervix starts to get thinner and stretch, ready for the birth, and in your case some of the blood vessels have broken—that's what caused the bleeding. Jane tells me you haven't lost a huge amount of blood, so I'm not too worried. We can keep an eye on you. The good news is that there's a really strong chance that we can deliver the babies as originally planned, at thirty-five weeks.'

'And the bad news?' Pippa asked.

'Jane tells me you were hoping for a normal delivery.' He took her hand and squeezed it. 'I'm sorry, we can't do that, because the placenta's going to be in the way. You could end up losing a lot of blood, and we just can't take that risk—for you or for the babies.'

A tear trickled down Pippa's cheek. 'I couldn't conceive normally and I can't even have a normal birth. I'm going to be a rubbish mother.'

'No, you're not,' Ed said. 'Lots of women need help with conceiving, and lots of women end up having a Caesarean. But the good news is that we can plan it, so you won't have to go through a trial of labour first, then end up in emergency surgery because the babies are in distress and you're exhausted. It's tough enough being a mum to twins without all that on top of it.' He smiled at her. 'Right now, I'd guess you're feeling disappointed and relieved and worried, all at the same time. In your shoes, I think I'd be bawling my eyes out. So I'd say you're doing just fine.'

Pippa bit her lip. 'So what now? I go home and have to rest?'

'No. We'd like to keep you on the ward,' Jane said, 'so we can keep an eye on you.'

'Overnight?'

Ed shook his head. 'Until you have the babies.'

'Three weeks? But—I can't.' Pippa looked horrified. 'I haven't sorted out the nursery yet! I only went on maternity leave last week.' She shook her head in distress. 'I've been so careful not to overdo things and rush around like I normally would. I've taken it really easy and waited for Mike to paint the walls instead of grabbing the step ladders and doing it myself. And now...' She rubbed a hand across her eyes, scrubbing away the tears. 'I don't want Mike's mother taking over and making the room what she thinks it should be like, instead of what I want.'

'Can your mum maybe step in and bat your corner for you?' Ed asked.

'No. She died from breast cancer, two years ago.' More tears slid down Pippa's cheeks. 'I wish she was here. I wish she was going to meet my babies. She would've been such a brilliant grandmother. She wouldn't take over and try to boss me around all the time, like Mike's mother does.'

'Ed, would you mind calling Mike for us while I sit with Pippa for a bit?' Jane asked.

'Sure.' Moving so that Pippa couldn't see his face, he mouthed, 'I'll give you a yell when he gets here and we'll talk to him.'

Jane sat with Pippa, holding her hand and soothing her until she'd calmed down. 'I know this is rough on you, but we can work round things. Ed and I are happy to talk to anyone you need us to, so they know exactly why you're in and that you need a bit of TLC.'

'I don't think Mike's mother knows how to give TLC,' Pippa said wearily. 'And he never stands up to her.'

'You'd be surprised how much it changes you, becoming a parent,' Jane said softly. 'Where you might not stand up for yourself, you suddenly find that you do for your children.' At least, you stood up for your favourite one. But Pippa didn't need Jane dumping her own inadequacies on her; she needed support.

Rosie, one of the midwives, came in. 'Jane,

sorry, Ed needs a quick word with you in his office.'

'Sure. I'll be back in a minute, Pippa.' She smiled at the midwife. 'Rosie, would you mind sitting with Pippa for a bit?'

'Of course I will.'

When Jane got to Ed's office, Mike Duffield was sitting on the chair at the side of Ed's desk.

'Jane, is Pippa all right? And the babies? Ed's just been telling me what happened. Can I see her?'

'They're all doing OK,' Jane reassured him. 'Mike, I know you're worried and you want to see Pippa, but we wanted a word with you before you go in.'

'Why? Is there something you haven't told her?'

Jane shook her head. 'We want to keep her in so we can keep an eye on her, and she's really upset about it.'

Mike frowned. 'So there *is* something wrong.'

'I've told you everything, Mike,' Ed said gently. 'We want to keep an eye on her because she might start bleeding again. We can monitor her and the babies here; if things get sticky and we need to deliver the twins, then there won't be any delay. Pippa's upset because she hasn't finished decorating the nursery.'

Mike's face cleared. 'Well, I can sort that out for her, and my mum will help.'

Just what Pippa had been afraid of. Jane steeled herself for a difficult conversation. 'Mike, there isn't an easy or tactful way to put this, and I apologise in advance if I'm stepping over the line here, but that's one of the things that's worrying Pippa—that she'll end up having the nursery your mum wants, not the one that *she* wants.'

Mike looked taken aback. 'You what?'

Ed glanced at Jane and gave a tiny nod. 'Is there a chance maybe you could talk to your mum?' he asked. 'Maybe you could tell her that Pippa's upset about being in hospital and not able to do things the way she wants, and ask her if she'd consider helping you carry out what Pippa planned. But most importantly she needs to come and see Pippa, to reassure her that it's going to be *her* choices that matter.'

'I…' Mike blew out a breath. 'To be honest, Mum and Pip tend to clash a bit. They both have strong ideas. If Mum thinks that Pip doesn't want her help, then it'll put her back up.'

And clearly Mike didn't relish being stuck in the middle. Jane's father was like that, so she understood exactly why Pippa hated the fact that Mike would never stand up for her. 'Is there someone else you can ask to help with the nursery? A friend, another relative?' Jane asked. 'Because Pippa needs to rest and be as calm as possible, for her sake and that of the babies. People who haven't gone through IVF often don't really understand the kind of emotional and physical strain it involves, and maybe your mum doesn't appreciate what Pippa's gone through.'

Mike grimaced. 'Mum doesn't actually know we had IVF. Pip didn't want her to know. She's got this thing about how people are going to think she's not a proper mum because she couldn't conceive without help.'

'She did say something like that,' Ed said, 'and I told her that of course she's going to be a good mum—it's got nothing to do with the way the babies were conceived or how they're going to come into the world.' He looked thoughtful. 'What about Pippa's dad? Or does she have a sister who can help?'

'Her dad's a bit frail, and her sister…' Mike wrinkled his nose. 'They're not close. I really don't think Pip would want me to ask her.'

Jane could appreciate that. She knew all about difficult sisters, too. Jenna would be the last person she'd ask for help—because she knew the answer would be no. 'What about her best friend? That's who I'd want to help me, if I were in Pippa's shoes. And if that would reassure Pippa, then as her doctor my advice to you would be to talk to her best friend.'

'Well, I could ring her,' Mike said slowly. 'Shelley's a bit bossy.'

'So's my best friend,' Jane said with a smile. 'It's one of the things I love about her. She gets things done.'

'All right. I'll call her,' Mike said. 'And I'll tell Pip not to worry about the nursery. I'll make sure it's how she wants it.'

'Thanks. Taking something big like that off her

mind will really help a lot. I'll take you through to her.'

Jane ended up spending the rest of the morning with the Duffields; when she went to collect her handbag from the rest room at the beginning of her lunch break, Ed was there, too.

'How's Pippa?' he asked.

'Much more settled. And thanks for having a word with Mike. That really helped.'

'Any time.' He smiled at her. 'Got time to have lunch with me?'

She shook her head regretfully. 'Sorry, I'm already meeting someone.' She glanced at her watch. 'And I'm going to be late! Gotta go. Catch you later.'

Jane didn't see Ed for the rest of the afternoon. She did a last check on her patients, making especially sure that Pippa had settled, at the end of her shift. She was about to leave the ward when she passed Ed's open door.

'Jane? Can I have a word?'

'Sure.'

'Close the door.'

She frowned, but did so.

'Tell me honestly, do I have a personal hygiene problem?'

She stared at him, puzzled. 'No. Why on earth would you think that?'

'Because, unless I'm also suffering from a bad case of paranoia, you seem to be avoiding me.' He sighed. 'Jane, I like you. And on Saturday I thought you liked me, too.'

She did. But she didn't want to risk getting hurt again.

Not knowing what to say, she stayed silent.

'So do I take it you've had time to think about it and you want to be strictly colleagues?' he asked.

'Yes.' She saw the disappointment in his eyes just before he masked it.

Oh. So he *did* really like her.

'And, if I'm really honest, no,' she admitted. 'Look, I don't want to go into details right now, but I don't exactly have a good track record when it comes to relationships.'

'Join the club. I'm divorced,' he said, surprising her. From what she'd seen of Ed, he was thoughtful and kind and charming. Not to mention the way he made her feel physically. So why on earth would someone want to break up with him? Unless he, too, had completely lousy judgement when it came to relationships, and had picked someone who really wasn't suited to him.

'I won't pry,' she promised.

'There isn't much to tell. We wanted different things.'

'I can identify with that,' she admitted. She'd wanted a family, and Shaun had wanted Jenna. 'Except I didn't get quite as far as marriage.'

'Sounds to me as if we have a lot in common,' Ed said. 'Including not wanting to get hurt. So how about it? We go for a pizza, somewhere really crowded with lots of bright lights, and I walk you home and kiss you very chastely goodnight outside your front door?'

'You actually want to go out with me?'

'Yes.'

He meant it. OK, so Jane's track record in judging men was pretty rubbish, but she'd seen the way he was with their patients. Totally sincere, kind, taking the time to listen. Ed Somers was a nice guy, as well as being the hottest man she'd ever met.

'Pizza, and a chaste kiss goodnight outside my front door,' she checked.

'There might be two chaste kisses. But I promise they'll be chaste. Unless—' there was a glint of mischief in his eyes '—you decide to kiss me unchastely. In which case all promises will be on hold.'

It was tempting. So very tempting.

Dared she trust him, let him get close to her? Maybe her best friend was right and she needed to just get out there, enjoy herself, and put the past behind her. Dating Ed, maybe ending up back in bed with him, didn't mean that she was going to fall in love with him. He'd been hurt, too. They didn't have to rush this or make any promises, just see where it took them. They could both enjoy this and keep their hearts intact.

'OK. I'd love to go for pizza.'

'Great. Give me five minutes to save this file and shut down the computer, and I'm all yours.'

All yours. Jane rather liked the sound of that. 'See you in five, then.'

CHAPTER SIX

JANE knew exactly the place to go: a small trattoria that was busy and brightly lit, and the food was fantastic.

'Excellent choice,' Ed said after his first taste of the pizza. 'The food's fantastic.'

'I normally come here with Sorcha—my best friend,' she explained. 'Because of the food.'

They spent the whole evening talking, discovering that they had similar tastes in music and books and films. And when Jane finished her third coffee and glanced at her watch, her eyes widened in surprise. 'Blimey! We've been here for four hours.'

Ed looked awkward. 'Sorry—I didn't mean to keep you that long.'

'No, I've really enjoyed it.' She was aware how surprised she sounded—and how bad that was. 'Sorry. I didn't mean to imply I thought I wouldn't enjoy your company. Just that it's been a while since I've gone on a date and I thought it might be a bit, well, awkward.'

'Snap. Except it wasn't,' Ed said softly. 'I've enjoyed tonight, too.'

He walked her home, escorted her up the steps to the entrance to her block of flats, and gave her a chaste kiss right at the corner of her mouth.

'Wasn't that meant to be my cheek?' Jane asked.

'Technically, it *is* your cheek,' he pointed out.

'Hmm.'

He kissed the other cheek, but this time Jane moved slightly and Ed ended up kissing her on the mouth. He pulled back and looked her straight in the eye. 'Jane, are you going to kiss me?'

'Would it be a problem?'

He smiled. 'No. It'd be a delight.'

And it was a delight for her, too. Hot enough to let her know that he found her attractive, but not so pushy that she felt pressured.

Finally, Ed broke the kiss. 'I'd better go back to the hotel.' He stroked her cheek. 'I'm not going to ask you to let me come in, even though I'd like to, because I don't quite trust myself to behave honourably.'

Was this his way of letting her down gently? she wondered.

He stole a kiss. 'You know, your face is really expressive. Never play poker, will you?'

Jane could feel her skin heat. 'Sorry,' she mumbled.

'This isn't because I don't want to come in, because I do. But we started this all the wrong way round. It might be a good idea to give us time to get to know each other properly, this time,' he said softly. 'See where it takes us.'

'I guess.'

His kiss was sweet and warm. 'See you tomorrow. Do any of your windows overlook the street?'

'The kitchen. Second floor, middle window.'

'Good. Put the light on and wave to me when you're in, OK?'

'OK.' Jane had never dated anyone who was quite that gentlemanly before. And she loved the fact that he actually waited until she was safely indoors and had waved to him before he sketched a salute back and left for his hotel.

'Mr Somers—do you have a moment?' Jane asked the following afternoon, leaning against the jamb of Ed's office door.

'Sure. Want me to come and see one of your mums?'

'No. I was just wondering, are you busy tonight?'

'No.' He looked pleased that she'd asked. 'What did you have in mind?'

'You said yesterday about watching a film. I was wondering, maybe you'd like to come over to my flat and see a film this evening. Say, about eight?'

'I'd like that,' he said.

'Comedy or serious drama?'

'I'll leave the choice to you.'

'You might regret that,' she warned.

He grinned. 'You said that about dancing with you. I didn't have any regrets then, so I doubt I'll have any regrets tonight, either.' He winked at her. 'See you later, Jane.'

* * *

At precisely eight o'clock, Ed walked up the steps to Jane's apartment block and pressed the buzzer.

'Come up. Second floor, first door on the left next to the stairs.' Her voice sounded slightly crackly through the intercom.

By the time he reached the second floor, her door was already open and she was waiting for him. 'Hi.'

'For you.' He handed her the flowers he'd bought on the way back to the hotel from the hospital.

'Oh, they're lovely, all summery and…' She buried her nose in them and inhaled deeply. 'I adore the smell of stocks. Thank you, Ed. They're gorgeous.'

'My pleasure.' He'd thought that roses might be too obvious, and was glad he'd opted for the pretty, scented summer flowers instead.

And he'd also guessed that she'd like crisp white wine. She beamed at him when he handed her the chilled bottle of Chablis. 'This is my favourite—and you really didn't have to, you know.'

'I know. I just wanted to.'

'Come in. I'm going to put these gorgeous flowers in water—make yourself at home,' she said. 'The living room's through there. I take it you'll have a glass of wine, too?'

'Thanks, that'd be lovely.'

Her flat was exactly what he'd expected it to be: small, but warm and homely. The living room had an overstuffed sofa and soft furnishings in rich autumnal colours. He couldn't resist browsing her bookshelves; there was an eclectic mix of thrillers, poetry and medical textbooks, and another shelf held a selection of films, a mixture of serious dramas and comedies.

On the mantelpiece there were several framed photographs. Ed knew he was snooping and Jane was cagey about her personal life, but he looked anyway. One of the photographs was of Jane on her graduation day with an older couple he guessed were her parents, though they didn't look much like her; another was of Jane with a bubbly-looking redhead he guessed was her best friend. There was also a photo of a much younger version of Jane with a Springer spaniel draped all over her and the widest, widest smile, and another of Jane with an elderly woman.

'Gorgeous dog,' he said when she came into the living room, carrying two glasses of wine.

'That's Bertie. He was my great-aunt's,' she said. 'I always wanted a dog, but my mum didn't really like them. She said they were too messy and she always moaned about dog hair on her clothes whenever we visited Sadie.' She shrugged. 'Sadie had a quiet word with me and told me that I could share Bertie with her, and she'd look after him between visits.'

'And I guess, working hospital hours and living in a flat, you can't really have a dog here,' he said.

'No.' She looked regretful. 'I adored Bertie. He was the sweetest, gentlest dog ever.'

'Is that Sadie?' he asked, pointing to the photograph of the elderly woman.

She nodded. 'Sadly, she died last year. But she was lovely. I was privileged to have her in my life.'

'That's how I feel about my sisters,' he said. 'And George.'

For a moment, he could've sworn that she flinched. And her smile didn't quite reach her eyes when she said, 'It's good to have people like that around.'

'Are these your parents?' He indicated the picture of her with the older couple.

'Yes.'

'And I'm asking too many questions?'

'No, it's OK.' She shrugged. 'It's an old picture now, but my mum's barely changed in the last thirty years. I guess that's the thing about supermodels—they have wonderful bone structure.'

'Your mum was a supermodel?'

She nodded. 'She's retired now.'

He studied the photograph, and it made him wonder. Jane's mother was classically beautiful, but there was something remote about her. Plus by Jane's own admission her mother was fussy about dog hairs and mud. He had the strongest feeling that Jane's childhood hadn't been anywhere near as happy as his own. He couldn't remember that much of his own mother, but his stepmother Frances had always been warm, welcoming and loving—not to mention completely unbothered about the amount of hair their assorted dogs and cats shed. Clearly Jane's mother wasn't like that; she didn't sound like the easiest of people to be close to.

'I think you have her eyes,' he said eventually, trying to be diplomatic.

'Maybe.' She handed him one of the wine glasses. 'Here.'

'Thanks.' He took the hint and put the photograph down. 'So what did you pick, in the end? Serious drama or a comedy?'

'Comedy,' she said.

'Sounds good.'

When she sat next to him on the sofa, he slid one arm round her shoulders and she relaxed into him. The film wasn't bad, but he couldn't take his attention off Jane. So much for his good intentions. But they'd spent hours talking last night, getting to know each other better. One kiss wouldn't hurt, would it?

He shifted slightly so he was half-lying on the sofa. When she leaned into him, he shifted further, and moved her so that she was lying on top of him.

'Hello,' he said softly, and reached up to kiss her.

He had meant it to be soft and sweet, but then

she opened her mouth, letting him deepen the kiss, and his control snapped. His fingers slid under the hem of her T-shirt, moving further up until his hands were splayed against her back. And the way she was lying, she'd be in no doubt of how much she turned him on. He could feel the softness of her breasts against his chest, and also the hardness of her nipples; so he had a pretty good idea that it was the same for her, too.

'Sorry. That wasn't meant to happen,' he said when they surfaced from the kiss. 'I was trying to be a gentleman. But you leaned into me.'

'Hmm,' she said.

But there was a twinkle in her eye, so he grinned back, moving so that he was sitting upright and she was still straddling him.

He wrapped his arms round her. 'You know what I was saying about taking it slowly and getting to know each other first? I've had a rethink.'

'And?'

'I reckon we need to do some speed dating.'

She frowned. 'Speed dating?'

'So we get to know everything about each

other. Like now. And then I can do...' He paused. 'What I think you'd like me to do, too.'

He loved the fact that she blushed spectacularly.

'Before I met you, I never behaved like this. For pity's sake, we haven't even known each other for a week,' she said.

'No. It's completely illogical and irrational... and irresistible.' He kissed her. 'Your eyes are very green.'

'What does that mean?'

'I noticed on Saturday. You know I said your eyes change colour? When you're turned on, your eyes go green.'

Her blush deepened even further. 'You make me sound like—I dunno, some kind of siren. I'm ordinary. Plain Jane.'

'If you were ordinary,' he said softly, 'I wouldn't be reacting like this to you.' He kissed her again, just to prove it. 'I was intending to go home. To be gentlemanly.'

'But?' Her voice was very, very soft.

'But what I really want to do right now is carry you to your bed and drive you as crazy as you drive me.' He shook his head. 'I don't do this sort of thing. I'm the serious one in the family, the one who plays by all the rules. But something about you makes me want to be different. To take a chance and follow my feelings instead of my head.'

'Like James Bond.' She stroked his face. 'You already know I think you'd give him a run for his money.'

Actually, he thought wryly, the James Bond-alike would be George, not him. 'Thank you for the compliment, but hardly.'

'Come off it. Half the hospital's swooning over you.'

'Since when?'

'I told you, the grapevine works fast at our place.'

He raised an eyebrow. 'Would you mind very much if they talked about us?'

She grimaced. 'I don't like being the hot topic.'

Of course. She'd probably been there after her ex. 'Did he work at the hospital?'

'No.' She sighed. 'I guess I ought to tell you what happened. Though it's not pretty. I came home early one day—I'd forgotten to tell him I was on a half-day—and found him in our bed with someone else.'

Ed sucked in a breath. How on earth could the guy have betrayed Jane like that? 'I'm sorry he hurt you like that. That's…' He couldn't find the words to describe it, but he needed to say something. To let her know he was on her side. 'That's a really shoddy way to treat someone.'

She shrugged. 'I'm over it now.'

'Are you?'

She nodded. 'But I will admit that Saturday was the first time I'd felt beautiful since it happened.'

'How long ago?'

'Eight months,' she admitted.

'Then I'm glad I could do that for you.' He paused. 'Just for the record, I don't believe in cheating. While I'm seeing you, I won't be seeing anyone else, and that's a promise.'

'Same here.'

'Good.' He stroked her hair. 'I don't know what to say.'

She shrugged. 'There's nothing to say. I

gave Shaun his ring back and moved out that same day.'

She'd been *engaged* to the guy when he'd cheated on her? What the hell had been wrong with him?

'Sorcha was brilliant and let me stay with her until I found this place.'

'The more you tell me about your best friend, the more I like her.'

Jane smiled. 'She's the sister I wish I had.'

'The best kind of friend. Since we're sharing difficult stuff, I should tell you…' He sighed. 'My family's, um, fairly well-to-do. And my ex thought she'd have the lifestyle that goes with that kind of family.' Camilla had come from the same kind of background as his own, and she'd had definite expectations. 'I don't think she realised the kind of hours that junior doctors work—or how important my job is to me. I think maybe she expected me to…' How could he put this without scaring Jane away? 'To give it up and join the family business,' he finished. He knew it was selfish of him, but he was truly glad that being the second son meant that he'd never had to face that choice—that he was able to follow his real calling and make a difference to people's lives, instead of doing his duty and trying not to let his family have any idea how trapped he felt.

He sighed. 'I guess I'm selfish. Or I didn't really love my ex enough, because I just couldn't give up medicine for her. Being a doctor, helping mums through tricky pregnancies and helping make their dreams of a family come true—that's who I *am*, not just what I do.'

She kissed him. 'That's how I feel about it, too.'

'But it's not fair of me to put all the blame on Camilla. I dragged her off to Glasgow because I had the chance to work with a top specialist and I wanted to take the opportunity to learn from him. It didn't occur to me how cut off she'd feel from London, and I should've taken her needs into account a lot more than I did,' he said. 'So I'm very, very far from being perfect.'

'You and me both,' she said softly. 'I had this dream and I was so sure that Shaun was the one to make it all come true for me. I expected too much from him. And I guess he couldn't take the fact that I was never going to be tall and skinny and elegant. So he found someone who was.'

'Which is incredibly shallow. It's not what people look like, it's who they are that's important. And anyway, not all men want a stick insect. Some men happen to like little, cute, curvy women.' He punctuated every adjective with a kiss. Just to make sure she knew he meant it. 'He really doesn't know what he's missing.' He kissed her again, and her hands slid into his hair. He splayed his palms over her spine. 'Jane. Shall we skip the rest of the film?'

Her eyes were very green. 'Yes.' She kissed him back.

He had no idea how they got off the sofa, but the next thing he knew he was on his feet, he'd scooped her into his arms, and he was carrying her out of the living room. 'Which one's your room?'

'First door on the right.'

He nudged the door open and smiled. 'I'm so glad you have a double bed.'

'It's good for spreading papers out on.'

'True.' He stole a kiss. 'But I have other plans.'

He set her down on her feet. 'Starting here.' He unbuttoned her jeans, and she sucked in a breath.

'I was in too much of a rush last time. This time I'm going to enjoy it.'

Her eyes widened. 'Ed—the curtains.'

'Wait here—and stop thinking,' he directed. He swiftly closed the curtains and switched on her bedside lamp, then came back to her side. Gently, he encouraged her to lift up her arms, and drew her T-shirt up over her head.

God, her curves made him ache. He didn't know whether he wanted to look at her first, touch her, taste her, or all three at once.

He dropped to his knees in front of her and gradually peeled her jeans down, stroking her skin as he bared it. He let her balance on him while he helped her out of the denim completely, then sat back on his haunches to look at her. 'Wow, you're gorgeous. All curves.'

She looked shy. 'Do you think you could take some of your clothes off as well? I'm feeling a bit…well, exposed, here.'

'I'm in your hands,' he said, standing up.

She peeled off his own T-shirt, then shyly undid

the button of his jeans. He helped her remove them, then traced the lacy edge of her bra. She shivered and tipped her head back in invitation. Smiling, he unsnapped her bra and cupped her breasts. 'You're gorgeous. Lush,' he whispered.

She coloured, but something in her expression told him that he'd pleased her.

Gently, he hooked his thumbs over the edge of her knickers and drew them down. She did the same with his boxers.

He picked her up, loving the feel of her skin against his, and laid her against the pillows. He paused to grab his wallet from his discarded jeans and ripped open the condom packet.

Her hand slid over his. 'My job, I think.'

It thrilled him that she'd refound her confidence with him—just as he was finding his with her. He shivered as she rolled the latex over his shaft. And then he was right where he wanted to be, kneeling between her thighs and buried deep inside her.

Her pupils widened with pleasure, and her eyes were the clearest green.

He took it as slowly as he could, until finally

her body tightened round his, pushing him into his own climax, and his body surged into hers.

Afterwards, Ed went to the bathroom, and returned to see Jane sitting in bed, looking slightly wary.

'I'm not expecting you to let me stay the night, but leaving right now would feel completely wrong,' he said. 'Can I stay for a bit longer?

She smiled. 'I'd like that.'

'Thank you.'

He climbed back into the bed and drew her into his arms; she held him close and he relaxed, enjoying the companionable silence and the warmth of her body against his. He waited until she'd fallen asleep, then wriggled out of the bed without waking her and dressed swiftly.

As he left the bedroom, he realised that the DVD player and TV were still on; they'd been so caught up in each other that neither of them had noticed. He turned them off, took their glasses into her kitchen, then took the top sheet from the jotter block next to the phone and left her a scribbled note propped against the kettle.

Hope you slept well. Can't wait to see you at work this morning. E x

Then he quietly let himself out of her flat.

CHAPTER SEVEN

THE note Ed had left her made Jane smile all the way through her hated early morning run and then all the way in to work.

When she walked into the staff kitchen, Ed was already there, spooning instant coffee into a mug.

'Good morning.'

He glanced round, gave her a sultry smile, and kissed her swiftly.

'Ed!' she said, shocked. 'Supposing someone had walked in on us?'

'They didn't,' he reassured her. 'Though would it really matter if they had?'

'I guess not. I mean, we're seeing each other, but we're both professional enough not to let it get in the way at work.'

'Exactly.' He smiled again. 'Good morning. Did you sleep well?'

'Yes. Did you?'

'Oh, yeah.' The expression in his eyes heated her blood. 'Especially as I had a very, *very* nice dream.'

'Funny, that. So did I.' She glanced at her watch. 'Rounds in ten minutes?'

'Suits me fine.' He gestured to the kettle. 'Want a coffee?'

'No, thanks. I'll pass.' She gave him a sidelong glance. 'I've already had coffee this morning. With a very nice side order.'

'You saw the note, then.'

'Indeed I did, Mr Somers.' And she loved the fact he couldn't wait to see her again. 'See you in ten.' She winked at him, and sashayed out of the kitchen.

Their rounds were routine; Pippa Duffield's condition was stable, and Mrs Taylor was responding so well to treatment that Ed planned to let her go home on Monday, provided she managed to continue eating little and often over the weekend.

But the afternoon saw Iris sending Rosie, one of the more junior midwives, to grab them both.

'Iris says she need a forceps delivery *right now*,' Rosie said. 'Prolapsed cord.'

Rare, and scary, Jane thought.

'And it's not a breech or a footling presentation.'

Rarer still. Jane looked at Ed, knowing how serious the situation could be; given that it wasn't a breech presentation, it meant that the umbilical cord was probably longer than normal and part of it had passed through the entrance to the uterus. There was a real risk of the blood flow being restricted during contractions so the baby wouldn't get enough oxygen, and the baby could be in distress—or even stillborn.

'How far down is the head?' Ed asked.

'The mum's in the second stage, fully dilated, and the head's pretty far down,' Rosie said.

'Too late for a section, then. OK. Iris is absolutely right. We'll need to try forceps,' Ed said, looking grim. 'But if the baby isn't out within three sets of traction, we're talking emergency section under a general.'

As soon as they went into the delivery suite, Iris introduced them to the mum, Tilly Gallagher, who was kneeling with her bottom in the air and her shoulders lowered to slow down the delivery. Iris was clearly following established procedure, pushing the baby's head back up between contractions to avoid extra pressure on the umbilical cord. Pushing the cord back behind the head wasn't an option, because handling the cord could cause the blood vessels to spasm and reduce the amount of oxygen coming to the baby.

Tilly's husband Ray was holding her hand and looking as if he wished he was elsewhere.

'Try not to panic, Tilly,' Ed said, 'but the umbilical cord's causing a bit of a complication and the safest way to deliver your baby is if we give you a little bit of help.' He glanced at Jane, who nodded and took over.

'We're going to use forceps to help deliver the baby. We'll also need to give you an episiotomy.' She talked Tilly and Ray through the procedure while Ed checked the monitor to see how the baby was doing and Rosie went to fetch one of the senior paediatricians, ready to check the baby over after delivery.

They helped Tilly into position for delivery, in

stirrups. 'I know it's not very dignified, but it'll help us deliver the baby quickly,' Jane said. 'Ray, if you'd like to stay here by Tilly's side, hold her hand and help her with her breathing?'

Ray looked grateful that they weren't expecting him to view the birth.

Ed administered a local anaesthetic and gave Tilly an episiotomy ready for the delivery. Jane put the forceps together and was about to hand them to him when he mouthed to her, 'It'll be good experience for you to do it.'

Prolapsed cords weren't that common, and Jane knew that he was right about this being good experience for her. Warmed that he had faith in her—and knowing that he would be there to help and advise her if things started to get tricky—Jane smiled at Tilly. 'OK. What I'm going to do is help guide the baby's head down with every contraction. If you're at all worried at any point, just say and we'll do our best to reassure you. Are you ready?'

Tilly took a deep breath. 'I'm ready.'

As Tilly's contractions progressed, Jane synchronised traction with the forceps, guiding the baby's head downwards. She was aware of Rhys Morgan coming into the delivery suite, but was concentrating too much on Tilly and the baby to exchange any pleasantries with him.

She was relieved when the baby was finally delivered; while Rhys and Iris checked the baby over, she and Ed checked Tilly over.

The baby was silent, and Jane was aware of every second passing, every pulse of blood in her veins.

Please let the baby cry. Please let them have been in time. Jane had her back to Iris and Rhys so she couldn't see what they were doing, but she knew they were probably giving the baby oxygen to help inflate the lungs and encourage the baby to breathe.

Please let the baby cry.

Just as she was starting to panic inwardly, she heard a thin wail.

At last. She exchanged a relieved glance with Ed.

She herd Iris calling out the Apgar score, and then finally Rhys came over with the baby wrapped in a warm blanket and placed the infant in Tilly's arms. 'Congratulations, Mr and Mrs Gallagher, you have a little boy.'

'Oh, my baby.' A tear slid down Tilly's cheek. 'Ray, he looks just like you.'

'He's— Oh, my God,' Ray whispered. 'Our baby.'

Jane couldn't hold back the tears trickling down her own face. 'He's gorgeous.'

'Congratulations,' Ed said warmly. 'There is a little bit of bruising, but that will go down in the next couple of days.'

'And he's going to be all right?' Ray asked.

'He's doing fine,' Rhys reassured her. 'The scary stuff is all past. I'll be in to see you later today, but in the meantime if you're worried about anything you're in very safe hands here.' He nodded acknowledgement to Ed and Jane. 'Catch you both later.'

Ed looked at Jane. 'You're crying.'

'I told you, I always do when I deliver a baby,' she said softly. 'Because it's such a perfect moment, the beginning of a new life, and it's such a privilege to be here.'

Iris put her arm round Jane and hugged her. 'You did well.'

'Hey. Tilly's the one who did most of the work, and your call was spot on,' Jane said.

'I just wish I'd picked it up earlier.' Iris sighed. 'But there were no signs, not until her waters broke and the monitor bleeped to say the baby was in distress.'

'Nobody could've predicted it. And your assessment was perfect,' Ed said.

He and Jane left Iris and Rosie with the Gallaghers and their newborn son, and Ed shepherded her through to his office. He opened the bottom drawer of his desk, extracted a bar of chocolate and handed it to her.

She blinked. 'What's this for?'

'Sugar. I think you need it.' He blew out a breath. 'That was a scary moment back then.'

'You're telling me.' She broke the chocolate bar in half and handed one piece back to him. 'I was getting a bit worried when I couldn't hear the baby crying.'

'Rhys says he's absolutely fine. They were lucky. And you were a star with the forceps.'

'Thanks for letting me do it. I mean, I've done forceps deliveries before, but they've been where the mum was so exhausted that she needed a bit of help.'

'This wasn't so much different. I knew you'd be fine—and if it had got tricky, I was there,' he said. 'We're a good team.'

Inside *and* outside work. Not that she should let herself fall for Ed too quickly. Even though she knew he wouldn't hurt her the way Shaun had, she also knew it wasn't sensible to rush into this.

'Are you busy tonight?' he asked.

'Don't think I'm pushing you away, but I'm studying.' Which was also a good excuse to keep him at just a tiny distance. Just enough to stop her being as vulnerable as she'd been with Shaun. 'Sorry. I did tell you I was nerdy. And boring.'

'No, you're being sensible and advancing your career. It's much better to study little and often than to cram it all in. You remember it better that way.'

'You're moving to your new flat tomorrow, aren't you?' she asked.

'Yes.'

'I could help, if you like,' she offered.

He smiled. 'I'd like that. Shall I pick you up at ten?'

'That'd be great.'

At precisely ten o'clock the next morning, Ed rang the entryphone, and Jane buzzed him up. Even dressed for moving and unpacking boxes, in soft ancient denims and a worn T-shirt, he looked utterly gorgeous.

'What?' he asked, tipping his head to one side.

She raised an eyebrow. 'Just thinking about Mr Bond.'

'Good.' His smile turned sultry. 'Hold on to that thought.'

'So do we need to go and pick up your things from a storage place?'

'I've already done that. The van's full,' he said. 'If I carry the boxes in, would you mind starting to unpack them?'

'Sure—actually, before we go, do you have coffee, milk and a kettle?'

He looked blank. 'It never even occurred to me.

I've been living in the hotel for a week, and my kettle's packed in one of the boxes.'

'So I take it you don't have any cleaning stuff, either?'

'I'm using an agency,' he admitted. 'They bring their own cleaning stuff. And they cleaned the flat for me yesterday. All we need to do is unpack.'

'I'll bring my kettle until we find yours,' she said. She grabbed a jar of coffee, took an opened carton of milk from the fridge, and emptied out her kettle. She put the lot in a plastic bag, locked the door behind her, and followed him outside. He opened the passenger door of the van for her, then drove her to a new apartment building in Pimlico, overlooking the river.

'Want to look round before we start?' he asked.

'Love to.' The flat was gorgeous, really light and airy. There was a large reception room with French doors, containing a couple of bookshelves, a small dining table and four chairs and two pale yellow leather sofas. Next to it was a decent-sized separate kitchen; there was a large bedroom overlooking the river, and an immaculate pure white bathroom. But the best bit for Jane was the river-side terrace leading off from the reception room.

'Oh, now this is gorgeous. You could have breakfast overlooking the river,' she said, gesturing to the wrought iron bistro table and chairs.

'That's what made me decide to rent it,' Ed said.

'If you had some tubs of plants out here for a bit of colour and scent, this balcony would be perfect,' she said. Not to mention eye-wateringly expensive; she knew what prices were like in this part of London, and the river view would add an extra chunk to the rent.

Ed had labelled his boxes sensibly, so it made unpacking much easier. He'd wrapped the crockery and glassware in newspaper to protect it for the move, so everything needed washing. 'Shall I do this while you put everything else where you want it?' she suggested.

By the end of the afternoon, Ed's flat looked a bit more lived-in. Though it was still very much a masculine bachelor pad; the soft furnishings were skimpy in the extreme, and the place had the air of being designed rather than being home.

'You're brilliant,' he said, kissing her. 'Thanks so much. I'd still be doing this at midnight if you hadn't helped.'

'That's OK.' But she was warmed by his appreciation.

She wandered over to the mantelpiece. 'Can I be nosey?'

'Sure.'

All the photographs were in proper silver frames, she noticed. And there was a really nice picture of him with a man who looked so much like him that he had to be Ed's older brother, plus three girls who had the same colouring but finer features and she guessed were his half-sisters. There was a very posh garden in the background; given the way they were dressed, she guessed that they'd been at some kind of garden party.

They all looked close-knit, with arms round each other and affectionate glances, and she suppressed a sigh. Ed was clearly close to his family. How could she explain to him that she wasn't particularly close to hers?

And she really, really didn't want to tell him

about Jenna. It had been hard enough telling him about Shaun.

'They look nice,' she said.

'They are. They're noisy and they're nosey and they drive me to distraction, but I love them to bits.'

The warmth in his voice told her that he meant it. Jane felt another pang. She loved her family, too, but they didn't make it easy for her. She'd thought for years that maybe she was the problem—the nerdy, quiet, clumsy one who didn't fit in. She had so little in common with them that it was hard for them even to like her, let alone love her.

But then she'd met Sorcha. The way Sorcha's family had taken her to their hearts, making her feel like one of them—plus the easy camaraderie she had with her colleagues on the ward—made her rethink the position. Maybe she wasn't the difficult one, after all. And you could still love someone without actually liking them, couldn't you?

'Penny for them?' Ed asked, obviously noticing her distraction.

No way. Wild horses wouldn't drag these thoughts from her. 'Nothing important,' she said.

To her relief, he changed the subject. 'How about I order us a takeaway? After making you slave all day, the least I can do is feed you.'

She smiled. 'Thanks. That'd be lovely.'

Jane spent Sunday studying. And it hadn't been as bad a week as she'd expected; nobody at the hospital had said a word to her about that awful article. Jenna had been remarkably quiet, too, though Jane supposed that her twin was probably busy on a shoot somewhere. It was when Jenna wasn't busy that trouble tended to happen.

And she ended up seeing Ed every other night for the next couple of weeks. He took her dancing; for the first time ever she found herself actually enjoying it, because he led her through the moves and was there to catch her before she fell. It turned out that he liked the same art-house cinema that she did; Shaun had always been bored if it wasn't an action flick, and he'd never discussed the films with her afterwards. Ed was different;

he insisted on going for an ice-cream sundae afterwards and talking about the film.

He whisked her off to Cambridge one Saturday afternoon, punted her all the way down the river to Grantchester Meadows, then lay in the long grass with her, her head pillowed on his chest. And when he kissed her in the middle of the river on the way back and whispered, 'You're beautiful,' she believed him. The more time she spent with him, the more she liked him; she'd never felt so in tune with someone before.

And maybe, just maybe, Ed was the one she could trust with her heart.

CHAPTER EIGHT

ON TUESDAY Jane was having lunch with Ed when his mobile phone rang.

'Excuse me a second,' he said. 'I'm going into the corridor where there's a better reception.'

He came back white-faced.

'What's wrong?' she asked.

He sighed heavily. 'That was Alice. George has had an accident.'

A road accident? And, given how pale Ed looked… 'Oh, no. Is he OK?'

'He'll live. Would you believe, he crashed into a cliff?'

She blinked. 'Into? Not off?'

'Into,' Ed confirmed. 'It wasn't a car accident.' He rolled his eyes. 'God knows what he was doing. Jet skiing or something like that, I suppose. He's going to be an inpatient for a week, at least. He'll be stir crazy by tonight, so I hate to think what he'll be like by the time the plaster comes off. He loathes being cooped up. The girls and I are going to have a rota to visit him, but he's still going to be bored rigid.'

'Is he in London?'

'Yes, over at the Hampstead Free—they're pinning his leg right now, so there's no point in me dropping everything and going over, because I can't be in Theatre with him.' He bit his lip. 'I'm going straight after work.'

He looked worried sick. Jane reached across the table and took his hand. 'Do you want me to come with you?'

He looked at her. 'It's a bit of an ask.'

'You'd do the same for me, if my brother had had an accident—not that I've got a brother, but you know what I mean.'

'Thanks, I appreciate it.' He grimaced. 'I'd better warn you in advance, George is a bit of a charmer and a terrible flirt. But I guess even he's going to be held back by having a broken leg and two broken wrists. Not to mention concussion.'

She squeezed his hand, guessing what he was worrying about. A bang on the head could turn out to be very, very nasty indeed; and, as a doctor, Ed would have a pretty good idea of the worst-case scenario. 'Don't build things up in your head. It might not be as bad as you think it is.'

'Yeah, that's the worst thing about being a medic. It's years since I did my emergency department rotation, but I remember seeing head injuries and—oh, God, if he ends up with a subdural haematoma or something...'

'You're building bridges to trouble,' she said gently. 'Alice has probably already told you the worst: a broken leg, two broken wrists and concussion. And, as you said yourself, right now there's nothing you can do.'

'No.' But Ed clearly felt too miserable to finish his lunch.

She was relieved mid-afternoon when they were called in to do an emergency Caesarean section, knowing that concentrating on their patient would take Ed's mind off his worries about his brother. She let Ed close the wound after delivery rather than asking to do it herself, knowing that he needed the distraction.

Finally, it was the end of their shift and they caught the Tube over to Hampstead. On the way, Ed responded to a stream of text messages from his sisters, father and stepmother. He paused when they got to the hospital shop. 'This is crazy, but I've got no idea what to take him. The girls have already stocked him up with grapes and chocolates, there's a no-flowers rule in place and George isn't exactly a flower person anyway.'

'Why not go and see him first?' Jane suggested. 'Then you can ask him what he wants you to bring in for him.'

'Good idea.' He grimaced. 'Sorry. I'm not usually this dense or indecisive.'

'Of course not. You're just worried about your brother.'

He hugged her. 'Thank you for being here—I do appreciate it. Even if I am being grumpy and unapproachable.'

She stroked his face. 'You're worried,' she repeated. 'Come on. Let's go up to the ward and see how he's doing. You'll feel a lot better then.'

'You're right.' He released her from the hug, but

twined his fingers through hers as they walked through the corridors. 'Thanks, Jane.'

'May I see George Somers, please?' Ed asked the nurse who was sorting out paperwork at the nurses' station.

'George?' The nurse looked up and then smiled at him. 'Oh, from the look of you, you must be his brother Ed. He's been talking about you.'

'How is he?'

'A bit sorry for himself, bless him,' she said. 'I'll take you through to see him.'

'Thank you.' Ed paused. He knew he was about to break protocol, but he really needed to know, because he was close to going crazy with worry. 'Can I be really cheeky and ask, would you mind me having a quick look at his notes, please? I'm not going to interfere with treatment or anything, but you know how it is when you're a medic.' He gave her an apologetic smile. 'You always start thinking the worst and worrying about the complications.'

'And seeing it all written down stops you panicking.' The nurse looked sympathetic. 'As long as George gives his permission for you to see them, yes—as long as you know that even then it'll be a favour, not a right.'

'Thanks. I won't abuse it,' Ed promised.

She took them through to the small room where George was lying on the bed, his eyes closed and his face covered in bruises.

Ed's fingers tightened round Jane's. Oh, God. He'd known on an intellectual level that George would be in a mess, but actually seeing it for himself made everything seem much more real. If George had been one of his patients, Ed would've coped just fine; he would've been brisk and cheerful and supportive. But seeing his older brother lying there after surgery, with all the associated tubes and dressings, made him feel as if he couldn't breathe. His lungs felt frozen with fear. What if there were post-op complications? What if there was a subdural haematoma they hadn't picked up? *What if George died?*

'Since he's asleep, is it OK to wait here until he wakes up?' he asked the nurse.

'Of course.' She patted his arm. 'Try not to

worry. He's doing fine. If you need anything, come and find me.'

Ed sat down on the chair next to George's bed and pulled Jane onto his lap. He really needed her warmth, right now. Thank God she had such a huge heart and wouldn't judge him.

'Do you want me to go and get you a cup of hot sweet tea from the café?' Jane asked.

'No, I'm fine,' he lied. More like, he didn't want her to move. He needed her close.

'You're not fine, Ed,' she said softly.

He sighed. 'I'm better with you here.' He leaned his head against her shoulder. 'Thanks for coming with me. And I'm sorry I'm such a mess right now.'

She stroked his hair. 'Hey. Anyone would be, in your shoes. It's always worse when it's one of your family lying in that hospital bed.'

'I hate to think of how much pain he's been in.' And the fact that George could've been killed... His brother's death would have left a huge, unfillable hole in his life. Not just his, either: his father, stepmother and sisters all loved George as much as Ed did, even when he was driving them crazy with one of his escapades.

He sighed. 'Why does my brother always have to take such stupid risks?'

'Wasn't stupid. Had protective gear on,' a slurred voice informed them.

Guilt rushed through Ed. George needed his rest, and his voice had been too loud. 'Sorry. I didn't mean to wake you.'

'Wasn't asleep. Just resting my eyes. Knew you'd be here.' George gave him a slightly sheepish smile. 'Alice already nagged me, so don't bother.'

'There's no point in nagging you. You won't listen anyway,' Ed said.

'Who's this?' George looked questioningly at Jane.

'Jane. Jane, this is my brother George.'

'She's sitting on your lap. Hmm. She the girl you wouldn't tell me about?'

Ed sighed. 'Yes.' He could see on Jane's face that she was wondering why he'd kept her quiet. Once she'd met his family, she'd understand: they were incredibly full on, and he wanted to be sure where this was going before he let her meet them. He'd explain later. But not in front of his brother.

''Lo, Jane,' George said.

'Hello, George. Nice to meet you, even though it's not in the best of circumstances,' she said politely.

'And you.' George smiled at her, and looked at Ed. 'Jane. Ex'lent. I can call you "Tarzan" now, Ed.'

Jane laughed. 'You can try, but he'll frown at you.'

George grinned. 'She knows you well, then.'

'Yeah, yeah.' Though it heartened Ed that George was feeling well enough to tease him. 'How are you feeling?'

'Bit woozy,' George admitted. 'Gave me enough painkillers to fell a horse.'

'Probably because you needed them, and you've had a general anaesthetic as well so you're going to feel woozy for a day or so.' Ed meant to be nice. He really did. But the fear turned to anger, and the question just burst out. 'What the hell did you do, dive-bomb the cliff or something?'

'No, got caught out by a gust of wind.'

'*Wind*? What the hell were you doing?'

'Paragliding.'

That was a new one on him. Though he knew that George had been looking for another outlet for his energy, since their father had banned him, absolutely, from racing cars.

'How did it happen?'

George grimaced. 'My fault. Not concentrating properly.'

Thinking of a girl, no doubt. 'You could've killed yourself, George.'

''M still here,' George said mildly.

'With what looks like a broken femur, two broken wrists and some broken fingers.' Ed sighed. 'Can I read your notes?'

'Yeah. Can you translate 'em for me?'

'Tomorrow, I will, when you're more with it,' Ed promised. 'Right now, you won't take much in—you're still too woozy even to string a sentence together properly.' And he really hoped it was the combination of pain and the after-effects of the anaesthetic making George slur his words, rather than being a warning signal of something more sinister.

He fished the notes out of the basket at the head of George's bed. 'Yup. Two broken wrists, one broken femur—and...' George had hit the cliff face on, and pretty hard. He'd automatically put his hands up to save his face, which was why both wrists and some fingers were broken; but he'd also damaged his leg. And he'd sustained a blow to his testes, according to the notes. Hard enough to put a question over his future fertility.

Which meant that, even though George was the heir to the barony, he might not be able to have children. And that in turn meant that at some point Ed could have to give up the job he loved and do his duty for the family. Not that that was uppermost in Ed's mind. All he could see was his brother crashing into the cliff. Lying on an ambulance trolley. On the table in Theatre. How nearly they'd lost him. 'You *idiot*. You could've killed yourself.'

George shrugged. ''M OK. Could be worse. Didn't break my head, did I?'

'No, just your leg and your wrists. I know you're a thrill-seeker, and I get that you love the adrenalin rush. But, for pity's sake, can't you do things the *safe* way?' Ed asked plaintively.

'Nagging.' George wrinkled his nose. 'Pointless.'

There were times when Ed really, really wanted to shake his older brother. But maybe not while he still had concussion. 'Give me strength.'

'Powered paragliding's not dangerous.'

'Says the man who's got a metal rod holding his leg together and both wrists in plaster.'

'What's powered paragliding?' Jane asked.

'Awesome,' George said, and smiled. ''S a motor like a backpack for take off, then you glide on the current. Show you pictures later.'

'I take it you need training to do that?' Ed asked.

'Yes. 'M certified.'

Jane smiled. 'Judging by the look on Ed's face, I think you might mean *certifiable*.'

George laughed. 'Prob'ly.' Then he sobered. 'Gonna be stuck here f'r a whole week.'

Given that George barely sat still for five minutes, this was going to crucify him, Ed thought. 'Think yourself lucky you're not in traction—

you'd be stuck there for a lot longer than that,' he said.

'What'm I gonna do for a whole *week*?' George asked plaintively.

'The girls and I will visit. And Dad and Frances.'

'You're working. Charlie and Bea've got exams. Alice'll nag me. Frances worries.' George sighed. 'Dad's fuming.'

Ed just bet he was. 'So am I,' he pointed out.

'Didn't do it on purpose.' George grimaced. 'Uh. A whole *week*.'

'There's the television,' Jane suggested.

'Can't switch channels.' He indicated his casts. 'Six weeks till the plaster comes off.' He grimaced. 'Can't wait to go home.'

Home? He seriously thought he was going to get up from his hospital bed and go *home*? Oh, for pity's sake. 'Be sensible about this, George. You're going to be here for at least a week. And you'll need physio on your leg and your shoulders when you leave here,' Ed warned. 'How exactly are you going to manage at home, anyway?'

George shrugged. 'Voice-controlled laptop. Don't need to type.'

'I didn't mean work.' Ed already knew his brother couldn't sit still at a desk; he paced his office and did everything with voice control. 'I meant with simple little things like washing, eating…going to the loo.'

'*Ed!*' George rolled his eyes. ''S a lady present.'

'I'm a doctor,' Jane said with a smile. 'I don't get embarrassed about bodily functions. And Ed does have a point. It's going to be hard for you to manage personal care with both wrists in plaster—and I'm not quite sure how you're going to manage a crutch, actually.'

'There's one very obvious solution,' Ed said. 'Come and stay with me until you're properly mobile again.'

'Not 'nuff room.'

'Yes, there is. I'll sleep on the sofa bed and you can have my bed—it'll be more comfy for you with your leg.'

'Thanks, bro.' George shook his head. 'But best not. We'd drive each other mad. You nag too much. I play too hard.' His face softened. 'Love you, Ed.'

Yeah. He knew. Because George had always been there for him. *Always*. George had read story after story to Ed in the nights when he couldn't get to sleep after their mum had left; and, twenty years later, his older brother was the one Ed had turned to after the night shift from hell, a miserable night that had caused him to question whether he was really cut out to be a doctor.

'I love you, too,' he said, his voice thick with emotion. 'But you give me grey hairs. I thought the oldest child was supposed to be the sensible one?'

George smiled. ''M sensible. Sometimes.'

Yeah. Ed knew. It was just the rest of the time.

'I just like doing—'

'—dangerous things,' Ed finished wryly. 'I know.' Though sometimes he wondered. Was George such a thrill-seeker because he was stuck as the heir to the barony and hated it? It was something they'd never, ever discussed. He'd always assumed that George was fine with it.

Maybe he was wrong. He'd been so wrapped up in his career that he hadn't even considered that George might've had a vocation, too. They needed to talk about this. Not right now, while George was still feeling rough from the crash and the anaesthetic, but soon. And maybe they could work something out between them.

'The girls said they'd already fixed you up with chocolates and grapes. What can I bring you?'

'Dunno. Can't do a lot with these.' George nodded at his casts, then grimaced. 'Feel sick.'

Jane slid off Ed's lap, grabbed a bowl and was just in time.

'Sorry. Not good to be sick over Ed's new girl,' George said sheepishly when he'd finished.

'Anaesthetic has that effect on people sometimes,' she said. 'Don't worry about it. I'm used to this sort of thing. Really.'

'Thank you. Still sorry, though.' George looked contrite.

She smiled. 'No worries.'

'Look, I'm going to see one of the nurses and ask if they can give you something for the sickness,' Ed said. 'Jane, would you mind staying with George until I get back?'

'Sure.'

'Sorry to be a nuisance,' George said when Ed had gone.

'You're not a nuisance. I think Ed's a lot happier now he's seen you for himself.' Jane gave him a rueful smile. 'It's just as well we had a busy afternoon, because he was going through all the possible complications in his head and worrying himself si—' Given that George was feeling queasy, that wouldn't be the best phrase, Jane decided, and changed it to 'Silly'.

George clearly guessed, because he smiled. 'Sharp. You'll be good for Ed.' He paused. 'Best brother I could ever have.'

'If it makes you feel any better, he feels the same about you,' Jane said.

'Yeah.' George closed his eyes. 'Sorry. Tired.'

'Hey, that's fine. Just rest. I'm not going anywhere—if you need anything, you just tell me, OK?'

''K,' George said.

Ed came back with one of the doctors, who gave George an anti-emetic and wrote it on the chart.

'Your brother really needs to get some rest now,' the doctor said.

'Of course.' Ed put an affectionate hand on his brother's shoulder. 'Reckon you can stay out of trouble until I see you tomorrow, George?'

'Can't go abseiling, can I?' George said lightly.

'I wouldn't put it past you,' Ed said. 'I'll be back tomorrow night after work. Do you want me to bring anything?'

'Chess set, maybe?' George asked. 'Move the pieces for me.'

'Sure. Get some rest, and I'll see you tomorrow.'

'You'll come back too, Jane?' George asked.

'Maybe not tomorrow—Ed might want some time with you on his own—but yes, I'll come back. And I'll play chess with you, if you like,' Jane said with a smile. 'Take care.'

Ed was silent all the way to the Tube station, and barely said a word until they got to her stop.

'I'll see you home,' he said.

Jane was perfectly capable of seeing herself home, but Ed was clearly upset and she was pretty sure he needed some company. 'Thanks.' She didn't push him into a conversation, but she noticed that he held her hand tightly all the way to her front door.

'Come up,' she said softly.

'I'm not going to be good company,' he warned.

'It doesn't matter.' She stroked his face. 'I hate to think of you going home and brooding. You saw something bad in his notes, didn't you?'

'It's not fair of me to discuss it.' He sighed. 'There's a potential problem, yes. Hopefully it'll sort itself out.'

'OK. I'm not going to push you to tell me. But if you do decide to talk, you know it won't go any further than me, right?'

'I do.' He kissed her lightly. 'And thank you.'

She put the kettle on and made herself a coffee and Ed a mug of tea, adding plenty of sugar.

He took one mouthful and almost choked. 'Jane, this is disgusting!'

'Hot sweet tea is good for shock.'

'Yeah.' He sighed. 'That's what George made

me drink, when I decided I couldn't be a doctor any more.'

She blinked. 'You were going to give up medicine?'

He nodded. 'I was on an emergency department rotation. There was a major pile-up, and—well, you know what a majax is like. I wasn't used to losing patients. Kids, some of them. And I just couldn't handle it.' He blew out a breath. 'When I got home the next morning, I knew George had been out partying all night and had probably only just crawled into bed, but he was the only one I could talk to about it. So I called him.'

'And he made you a mug of tea like this?'

'Yeah. He came straight over and cooked me a fry-up.' He smiled wryly. 'George is a terrible cook. The bacon was burned and the eggs were leathery. I had to cover everything in ketchup to force it down. But it was the best breakfast I've ever had. He made me talk until it was all out. And then he told me it was just one shift in a department that wasn't right for me, and if I gave up medicine I'd regret it and I'd make everyone around me miserable. He said I'd be a great doctor, as long as I found the right department for me.'

There was a huge lump in Jane's throat. What must it be like to have a sibling who supported you like that, instead of taking and taking and taking all the time? 'He was right,' she said softly.

'Yeah.'

'And he's in good hands. The Hampstead Free has a really good reputation.'

'I know.' Ed sighed. 'It's just...'

'He's your brother. And you worry about him.' She walked over to stand behind him and slid her arms round his neck. 'I don't have the right stuff in the fridge to cook you a fry-up, but I have the makings of other comfort food. Like a toasted cheese sandwich.'

'Thanks, but I'm not sure I could eat anything.'

'Trust me, some carbs will help you feel better.'

He lifted her hand to his mouth and kissed her palm. 'You're wonderful. I hope you know that.'

'Sure I do,' she said. She kept her voice light, but the fact that he felt like that about her made her feel warm from the inside out.

'I'm not sure I could've got through seeing George like that without you there.'

She gave a dismissive shrug. 'Of course you would.'

'But you made it better. Only you,' he said softly.

'Hey.' She kissed him lightly, and busied herself making toasted sandwiches before she did something really stupid—like telling him she thought he was pretty wonderful, too.

'George liked you,' Ed said. 'Though he's going to torment me about the Tarzan thing. As soon as his hands have stopped hurting, he's going to start beating his chest and doing the yell.'

'And are you telling me you wouldn't do the same to him, if he was seeing a girl called Jane?'

Ed looked faintly sheepish, and she laughed. 'He's very like you, you know.'

'Apart from being in plaster and covered in bruises, you mean?'

'No. I mean, he's like you but without the brakes. He must drive his girlfriends crazy with worry.'

'Not to mention his parents and his siblings,'

Ed said dryly. 'He did go through a spell of racing cars, but Dad had a word with him.'

'And that stopped him?'

'Surprisingly, yes.' Ed frowned. 'He wouldn't tell me what Dad said to him, but it must've been pretty tough.'

'So he's always done dangerous sports and what have you?'

Ed nodded. 'You know you were saying I remind you of James Bond? That's actually how George is. He thinks nothing of skiing down a double black diamond run.'

'As I know nothing about skiing, I take that means it's a really hard one?' Jane asked.

'Yes. But he's been crazier these last six months,' Ed said thoughtfully. 'He's taken a lot more risks.'

'Did something happen six months ago?'

Ed thought about it. 'Yes. I should've made him talk to me. But I guess I was still getting over the divorce and I wasn't paying enough attention.' He sighed. 'Now he's stuck in a hospital bed, he's not going to have any choice—he'll have to talk to me. And maybe I can help him sort out whatever's going on in his head.'

Ed relaxed more after they'd eaten, though he seemed more comfortable in the kitchen than anywhere else, so Jane didn't suggest moving. Eventually, he squeezed her hand. 'You were going to study tonight. I'd better go. I've held you up long enough.'

'It's OK. I can catch up some other time—it's not as if I've skipped studying for weeks on end,' she said lightly. He looked so lost. She couldn't possibly make him go back to his flat where he'd be on his own, brooding and worrying all night. 'I think tonight you could do with not being on your own. So if you want to stay…' She took a deep breath. 'There are no strings. Just—if you want to stay, you're welcome.'

'I'd like that. I'll have to leave at the crack of dawn so I can get some clean clothes before work, but if you're sure?'

She smiled. 'I'm sure.'

CHAPTER NINE

ED LAY awake; he was brooding, but not as much as he would've done had he been alone in his flat. Jane was sprawled all over him and it just felt better, being here with her. She had a huge heart and, even though he guessed that asking him to stay had put her in a vulnerable position, she'd seen exactly what he needed and hadn't hesitated to offer.

He held her closer and, in response, her arms tightened round him.

Their lovemaking that night had been so sweet, so tender, and he felt that Jane really understood him—far more than anyone he'd dated before. OK, so they'd only known each other for a month, but it was long enough for him to have worked out that there was something special about her. Not just the calm, confident way she was with people at work, treating everyone with respect and kindness. Not just the physical stuff that made his heart beat faster. He liked her instinctively. He'd never felt so in tune with someone like this before. And he really hadn't expected to fall for someone so fast.

He couldn't tell her. Not yet. She'd come out of her shell a lot with him, but even so he didn't want to take this too fast for her and risk her backing off again. But he was starting to hope that this was more than just a rebound fling— for both of them.

The next morning, Ed woke early; for a moment, he was disorientated, but then he remembered where he was. In Jane's flat. In Jane's arms.

Last night, he'd leaned on her. This morning, it was time to even up the balance. He gently disentangled himself from her arms, climbed out of bed and made coffee for them both.

'Thank you for last night. For being there,' he said softly, kissing her as he climbed back into bed.

'It's no problem. You would've done the same for me,' she said.

'Of course I would. You're on the list of people who could call me at three in the morning and I wouldn't yell at you for waking me up—I'd come straight to your side. And it's not that big a list,' he said. His parents, his siblings and his very closest friends. And Jane.

She smiled. 'Snap.'

Funny how something so simple as drinking coffee in bed with her made his world seem brighter. He finished his coffee. 'I'd better go back to my flat and get some clean clothes, but I'll see you at work, OK?'

'OK. And if you're not busy at lunchtime,' Jane said, 'perhaps you might like to have lunch with Sorcha and me.'

He realised immediately what she was saying. Yesterday, he'd asked her to meet the closest person to him; and now she was returning the compliment. Letting him that little bit closer. 'I'd like that,' he said simply. 'Very much.'

The ward was incredibly busy, that morning; Jane called Ed in to help her with a difficult delivery.

'Just after his head emerged, his neck retracted and his cheeks puffed out.'

It was a classic symptom of shoulder dystocia, where the baby's shoulder was caught on the mother's pubic bone so they couldn't deliver the baby.

'Is the baby big for his dates?' Ed asked.

'And ten days overdue. But there weren't any indications that it was going to be a problem.'

Shoulder dystocia was always a tricky situation, with the risk of the baby dying during delivery from not getting enough oxygen. Even if the baby was delivered alive, there was still a risk of a fractured collarbone or damage to the nerves in the baby's neck.

Quickly, Jane introduced Ed to the mum and her partner and explained the situation to them.

'If we can change your position,' Ed said, 'it'll move your pubic bone and that should give us enough leeway to deliver the baby safely. Try not to push just yet, OK?'

'OK.'

Gently, he and Jane guided the mum onto her

back, with her bottom to the edge of the bed and her thighs guided back towards her abdomen.

'Jane, do you know the Rubin manoeuvre?' he asked.

'I know the theory.'

'Great.' Though it meant that she'd yet to put it into practice. Well, that was what he was here for. He directed her where to put suprapubic pressure over the baby's anterior shoulder so it moved towards his chest and would slip free. 'I'll tell you when to press,' he said. 'Rosie, can you get the neonatologist down?' This baby would definitely need careful checking over in case of nerve damage or fractures.

He really, really hoped the manoeuvre would work; otherwise, given that the mum already had an epidural and wasn't mobile, it would mean giving her an episiotomy and moving to more advanced intervention.

At the next contraction, he said, 'Now,' and gradually applied traction to the baby's head.

To his relief, it worked, and the baby finally slipped out.

'Well done,' Ed said to the mum.

The neonataologist checked the baby over, then came over with a broad smile and gave the baby to the mum for a cuddle. 'I'm pleased to say that he's a very healthy little boy—he had a bit of a tough time coming into the world, but he's absolutely fine.'

Ed and Jane exchanged a loaded glance. The outcome could have been so very different. Luck had definitely been on their side.

The mum was in tears of relief. 'Oh, my baby.' She looked at Ed. 'Thank you both so much.'

'It's what we're here for. Congratulations,' Ed said with a smile.

'He's gorgeous,' Jane added. She stroked the baby's cheek, then wiped the tears away from her own. 'Sorry. Newborns always make me cry. They're so perfect.'

'I think I need some sugar after that,' Ed said.

'Me, too.' Jane blew out a breath. 'That was a scary one. Thanks for talking me through it.'

'I barely needed to do that—you already knew the theory.'

'Which isn't *quite* the same as doing it in practice, knowing what could happen if you get it wrong.'

'But you got it right. And you're a quick learner—you won't need a word from me next time.'

'Hopefully not.' Jane glanced at her watch. 'Perfect timing. Lunch.'

In the canteen, a gorgeous redhead was already waiting for them—a woman Ed recognised from the photograph in Jane's flat.

'Caught up in the delivery room?' she asked.

'Yup. And it was a scary one.' Jane introduced them swiftly. 'Sorcha, this is Ed, our new consultant; Ed, this is Sorcha, my best friend—she's a rheumatologist.'

'I hope you don't mind me gate-crashing your lunch,' Ed said, shaking Sorcha's hand.

'Not at all. It's nice to meet you,' Sorcha said.

During lunch, Ed could see her watching him and trying to work out what his relationship with Jane was—whether it was strictly work, or if there was more to it than that. So had Jane been keeping him as quiet as he'd been keeping her? he wondered. And for the same reason?

He could see the second that Sorcha worked it out. Because she smiled very sweetly at her best friend. 'I am *so* desperate for a cappuccino. And a tiny, tiny bar of chocolate.'

'And it's my turn to fetch the coffee,' Jane said, getting up. 'OK. See you in a second.'

'So how long have you been seeing Jane?' Sorcha asked when Jane was out of earshot.

'Seeing her?' Ed asked.

She sighed. 'Don't play games. It's obvious in the way you look at each other—apart from the fact that she already knows exactly how you take your coffee and whether you're a chocolate fiend or not. I noticed she didn't even need to ask you what you wanted.'

'Right. Not long.'

Sorcha's eyes narrowed. 'I see. And this is a casual thing, is it?'

Well, if she was going to be that open with him, he'd give her the same courtesy. 'No, I don't think it is. And I'm glad she has someone to look out for her. My brother was still woozy from anaesthetic when he met her last night, or he would've been asking exactly the same questions. And, believe you me, my sisters are going to be every bit as careful as you when they meet her.'

'You're close to your family?'

'Yes. My family's great.'

Sorcha looked approving. 'Jane's like a sister to me.'

'So she told me.'

'She's got the biggest heart in the world,' Sorcha said, her gaze challenging.

'Absolutely.' He knew that first hand.

'And she's vulnerable.'

He knew that, too. 'Thanks to Shaun.'

'*Him*.' She rolled her eyes. 'I tell you, if he had a heart, I'd be first in the queue to remove it with a rusty spoon.'

Ed got the message. Very firmly. Hurt Jane, and Sorcha would be on the warpath.

'So she actually told you about him?'

'Yes.' He could see in Sorcha's face that she hadn't expected that. Clearly Jane didn't usually talk about what had happened. 'Look, I know Jane's special. I'll be careful with her, Sorcha. You don't have to worry.'

'Good.' Sorcha bit her lip. 'I can't believe she actually told you about Shaun and J—'

'OK, Sorcha, you can stop doing the guard dog act now,' Jane cut in, carrying a tray with three mugs of coffee. 'Sorry, Ed.'

'Nothing to apologise for. I think Sorcha and I understand each other. Which is a good thing. We know we're on the same side.' He held Jane's gaze. 'Yours.'

'Thank you. I think. But no more discussing me, OK?'

'Unless we need to,' Sorcha said.

Ed laughed. 'I'm so tempted to introduce you to my brother, Sorcha. I think you might be the only woman in the world who'd have the ability to keep him under control.'

'Too late. She's already spoken for,' Jane said.

'Shame. You don't happen to have a clone?' he asked Sorcha hopefully.

Sorcha laughed. 'No. But I think you and I are going to be friends.'

Jane didn't go with Ed to visit George that evening, knowing that he needed some time alone with his brother so he could start persuading George to open up about whatever was bothering him. But she made it clear that Ed was welcome to drop in on his way home if he needed a hug and someone to talk to. As always, a hug turned to something more, and Ed ended up staying the night again. And she somehow ended up staying at his flat after they'd visited George on Friday night.

This was all going crazily fast; and yet she trusted Ed instinctively. She knew he wouldn't hurt her. He wasn't like Shaun. He had integrity, he thought of others and he learned from his mistakes.

On Monday, she had a day off, and dropped in to see George in the morning.

'I thought you could do with a fresh challenger at chess,' she said.

'Janey! How lovely to see you.' He brightened when he saw what she was carrying. 'Are they for me?'

'Yup. Fresh English strawberries. And I've already washed and hulled them.'

'Oh, wow. Has anyone told you lately that

you're wonderful?' Then he looked at his hands. 'Um, think they might be a bit cross with me if I get the casts covered in strawberry juice, and I'm not very good with cutlery right now.'

'No. Breaking your wrists *and* your fingers is pretty harsh.' She produced a spoon. 'Bearing in mind that I'm a doctor, I think it might be OK for me to feed them to you. As I would do for any of my patients if they were in this state.'

'I don't expect any of your patients would end up with all these breaks,' he said.

'Not usually, though I did once deliver a baby where the mum had a broken ankle,' she said with a smile, and set up the chess board on the table that slotted over his bed. 'And I'd better check before I give you these—you're not allergic to strawberries, are you?'

'No. And I *love* strawberries. Thank you.'

She sat on the edge of the bed, so it would be easier for her to move the chess pieces according to his directions, and fed him the strawberries.

'I can see why Ed's so taken with you,' he said when she'd finished. 'He tends to be a bit cagey about letting us meet his girlfriends. Probably because we're all so full on and we've been nagging him about…' His voice tailed off. 'I'll shut up. I was about to be really tactless.'

'Nagging him about it being time he got a life after his divorce?' Jane asked.

George raised his eyebrows. 'He told you about Camilla?'

'Yes.'

He blew out a breath. 'I told him he was making a huge mistake, but she'd told him she was pregnant, and Ed *always* does the right thing—so he married her.'

'Pregnant?' Ed hadn't told her that bit.

It must have shown in her expression, because George grimaced. 'So he didn't tell you everything. Sorry. I didn't mean to be tactless.'

'That's OK. So are you telling me that Ed has a child?' But there hadn't been any photographs of a baby in his flat. He hadn't mentioned a child. And she just couldn't see Ed turning his back on his child. He wasn't that kind of man.

'No. She lost the baby just after they got married.' George left a very significant pause. 'Or so she said.'

Ah. Now Jane understood. And she was relieved that she hadn't been wrong about Ed. 'And you think she was lying to him in the first place, to get him to marry her?'

George nodded. 'Even though she was from the same kind of background as us, they really weren't suited. She wanted different things and she definitely didn't want to be a doctor's wife. But Ed thinks it was all his fault for not giving her the life of luxury she wanted, and he's been wearing a hair shirt ever since.' He looked at her. 'You've been good for him. You're definitely helping him lighten up.'

Jane couldn't help laughing. 'That's so ironic.'

'How come?'

'They used to called me "Plain Jane, Super-Brain" at school.' Jenna had managed to get the whole school to chant that one. Especially the popular crowd she hung around with; Jane's refusal to wear a ton of make-up or give up her studies to fit in with them had gone down very, very badly.

'So you're a nerd? Nerdy's good,' George said

with a smile. 'My sisters are all nerds. Have you met the girls yet?'

'No.'

'You'll like them. They boss Ed around, and he...' George grinned. 'Well, he just lets them. He's putty in their hands.'

She could just imagine it. And she'd just bet that the girls adored both their brothers. 'Do they boss you about?'

'They try—but, until one of them can beat me down a double black diamond ski run, they're not going to get very far.'

She laughed. 'Right now, even I could beat you down a nursery ski slope. You can't ski when you've got a pin in your leg.'

'Tell me about it.' He rolled his eyes, looking disgusted. 'The doctor said I can't ski until the end of the year, at least. Ed says they'll take the pin out when I'm healed, because I'm under forty.'

'Ed's been, how shall I put this?' She gave him a wicked smile. 'Well, he's been boning up on orthopaedics.'

George laughed. 'Oh, I *love* that you do bad

puns. So will Charlotte. Actually, the girls will all love you.'

To be part of a big, noisy, warm, close family… Jane would give a lot for that. But she knew she was already presuming far too much. She and Ed had known each other for only a month. Yes, they were getting on well. Really well. But, given her track record in relationships, she'd be foolish to let herself hope for too much.

She pushed the thought away. 'Have you met your physio yet?'

George grimaced. 'Yes. He made me get up and walk about the day after the op.'

'Absolutely. You need to keep you moving so your muscles don't seize up—it's going to drive you mad, but you really need to do what he says, to save yourself a lot of pain and hard work in the future.'

'I can follow directions, you know.'

'Can you?' she asked.

He gave her a rueful smile. 'OK, so I like to run my own life.'

'At a hundred miles an hour.'

He laughed. 'That Queen song was made for

me.' He sang a couple of bars from the chorus of 'Don't Stop Me Now'.

'I think you might be right.' She smiled back at him.

'I'm glad Ed's met you. You're definitely more his type than the debutantes who used to throw themselves at him.'

'Debutantes?' What debutantes?

George frowned. 'You mean he hasn't told you?'

'Told me what?'

'Forget I said anything,' he said hastily.

'No. Especially as you're in check. Told me what?'

He ignored the chessboard. 'What do you call him at work?'

'Ed.'

'No, I mean, do you call him Dr Somers?'

'No, he's a qualified surgeon. He's a Mr.'

'Uh-huh.' George paused. 'Did he tell you what I do for a living?'

'He said you're in the family business.' And that his family was well-to-do, though Jane hadn't paid any real attention to that. It was Ed she found attractive, not his bank account.

'I am. But I'm guessing he didn't tell you what the business was.'

She frowned. 'No.'

'I'm learning to run the estate. Which comes with a country pile whose roof just *eats* money.' He paused. 'And, as the eldest son, that makes me heir to the barony as well as being the future custodian of said money-eating roof.'

Barony? Jane felt the colour drain from her face. Their father was a baron. Which meant that Ed, George and their sisters would all be targets for the paparazzi. The kind of people *Celebrity Life* was desperate to run stories about—the magazine that had judged her so very harshly, just recently.

George's eyes widened with dismay. 'Oh, God, I've really messed things up now, haven't I?'

'No.' She dragged in a breath. 'I suppose you get snapped a lot by the paparazzi.'

'Usually doing something dashing, with my arm around a leggy blonde,' George said ruefully. 'I'm afraid I'm a bit of a stereotype. Well,

I hope there's more to me than that, but that's how the press sees me. The playboy with a taste for blondes.'

Jane thought of Jenna, and felt sick.

As if he guessed part of what was worrying her, he said softly, 'Jane, they tend to leave the rest of the tribe alone. They're scared Alice will skewer them in court. Bea's learned to turn it round so they end up being wowed by her architecture instead of her private life and give her the right sort of column centimetres. And Charlotte...well, she just speaks Latin to them and they don't understand a thing she says, so they can't get a story out of her. And Ed, they can't work out at all. The only stories they can dig up about him tend to be him as the hero doctor, and he downplays it, so they can't get a quote. Honestly, it's just me they go for, normally.'

'So am I going to get snapped on my way out of here, because I'm visiting you?'

'I very much doubt it,' he said. 'I can hardly do anything scandalous with both wrists in plaster and a pinned leg.'

'Oh, I think you could.'

He smiled. 'Teasing me back—I like that. You'll fit in to the family just fine.'

'Ed and I are just good friends.'

'Are you, hell. I haven't seen him like this about anyone, and that includes Camilla. He moons about you.'

She rolled her eyes. 'No, he doesn't.'

'Yes, he does, when you're not with him. And that's good.' George looked solemn, for once. 'I worry about him being too serious, and he's way too hard on himself.'

'He worries about you going too far.'

'I might have learned my lesson. Almost a week of being stuck in here has given me an awful lot of time to do nothing but think.'

'So you're going to settle down? Every cloud has a silver lining, hmm?'

'Something like that. He's serious about you, Jane. Don't hurt him. He's a good man—the very best.'

'I know.'

'You're in love with him, aren't you?'

No way was she admitting to her feelings. 'Can

we change the subject? And, by the way, you're in check again.'

'Why didn't you warn me how good you are at chess?' George grumbled. But to her relief he changed the subject, and the conversation stayed light for the rest of her visit.

That evening, Ed said, 'You've made a real hit.'

'How do you mean?'

'George. It was your day off, and I gather you spent half of it playing chess with him. And you took him strawberries. Hand-fed them to him, I hear.'

'Well, he can hardly feed himself, given that his fingers are splinted and his wrists are in plaster as well. Wielding a spoon for him isn't a big deal.' She paused. 'Do you mind?'

'No.' Though he didn't meet her eye. 'George talks a lot,' he muttered.

So that was what was bothering him. He was worried that George had told her things he'd left out. Which was pretty much the case, she had to admit. She brought Ed's hand up to her mouth and kissed his palm, then curled his fingers round the kiss. 'He told me a lot about you. Probably things you'd rather I didn't know, and I'm not breaking his confidence. But I can tell you that he really loves you.' And she'd guess it would be the same with his sisters and his parents. How she envied him that. Knowing that he was loved for being himself.

She paused. 'So when were you going to tell me what the family business was?'

Ed grimaced. 'Sorry. I know I should've said something to you myself. But...how do you tell someone that you're the son of a baron, without sounding as if you're a huge show-off?'

'The same way you do when your mother used to be a supermodel thirty years ago.' She shrugged. 'So do I need to start watching out for paparazzi?' That was the one thing that had really worried her. George had said it wouldn't be a problem, but she couldn't imagine George being upset by the press, the way she was. Ed knew her better—not well enough to know about the reasons why, but he'd guess that her childhood had been partly in the spotlight because of her mother. And not always in a good way.

'No, you don't need to worry about them,' Ed confirmed. 'Something you should know,' she said carefully. 'I'm really not good with paparazzi.'

'They must've been so intrusive when you were young, with your mum being a model.'

'Something like that.' She knew she ought to tell him about Jenna, about the article and the full story about what had happened with Shaun—but she just couldn't bear to see the pity in his eyes.

'I'm only the second son. They're not interested in me,' Ed said, kissing her. 'I'm boring Mr Edward Somers, consultant obstetrician, who doesn't even have a private practice delivering babies to the stars and minor royalty. So they leave me alone. George is far more interesting.' He sighed. 'Sometimes I think that George only does what he does to draw their fire away from us. But I could put up with a bit of annoyance from the paparazzi if it meant he'd stay in one piece.'

The following evening saw Ed sitting at George's bedside. 'I gather you ratted me out to Jane.'

'Ah. Sorry about that.' George looked faintly guilty. 'When she said you'd told her about Camilla, I thought you'd told her the lot. Including about the baby.'

Ed blew out a breath. 'Oh, *great*. She didn't mention that.'

'Because she's tactful and I talk too much.'

'Actually, no, you don't talk enough,' Ed said, seizing the opening.

'Why do I get the distinct impression that I'm not going to like this conversation?' George asked.

'Because I want you to tell me what's wrong.'

'Nothing's wrong. I'm just grumpy about having to be more sedate than I usually am.'

'No, I mean before that.' Ed paused. 'I've been thinking. Are you feeling trapped?'

'In this hospital bed, and knowing I can't drive for weeks?' George rolled his eyes. '*Totally.*'

'I mean trapped by all the expectations on you. You've grown up knowing everyone expects you to take over from Dad. But if there's something else you'd rather do—maybe there's something we can work out.'

George shook his head. 'Ed, you don't have to worry about that. It's not the barony stuff. I'm just an adrenalin junkie, that's all. I'm fine with taking over from Dad. Actually, I'm beginning to see what he likes about managing the estate.'

'Really?'

'Really,' George confirmed.

'And you'd tell me if something was wrong? Even if I couldn't help you fix it, I'm always here to listen. You know that, don't you?'

'Of course I do. Just as I'm here for you, Tarzan.' George raised an eyebrow. 'You're serious about Jane, aren't you?'

'Don't try to change the subject.'

'I like her,' George said. 'She gets what makes you tick. She wouldn't make you miserable, like Camilla did.'

'That's not fair, George. I made Camilla just as miserable as she made me.'

'But you're taking the blame for it. And that's not fair either. She trapped you into marriage. She lied her face off, knowing you'd do the right thing by her.'

Ed waved a dismissive hand, not wanting to

talk about it. Or about how much he'd loved the idea of being a father. Or how something in him had broken when Camilla had made it very clear that she didn't want to try making another baby, and he realised he'd married completely the wrong woman for him. 'I still think something's up. Something you're not telling me.'

George just laughed. 'You'll turn into a conspiracy theorist next! I'm fine. Let's set up the chess board.'

He wasn't fine, Ed thought. But clearly his brother wasn't ready to open up yet. Ed had a strong suspicion that it was something to do with their mother and the meeting George had had with her solicitor, but he was just going to have to wait until George was ready to talk. And when he was ready, Ed would make sure he was there.

CHAPTER TEN

'I KNOW it's a big ask, and it's not really a "come and meet the folks" thing,' Ed said on the Friday night. 'George is bored out of his mind, you're the only person who's managed to beat him at chess in five years, and he's desperate for a re-match.'

'And it's going to be easier for us to go and visit him than for you to bundle him into your car and bring him here, especially as he's probably not going to be too comfortable in a car,' Jane finished.

Ed looked relieved that she understood his worries. 'Yes.'

'So is your whole family going to be there?' she asked.

'Um, yes. George is staying with our parents until he's out of plaster. But I'll tell them to back off and keep their questions to themselves. And there won't be any paparazzi. Though I can guarantee that lunch will be good—Frances is a fantastic cook.' He looked beseechingly at her. 'So will you come with me on Sunday?'

To meet the rest of Ed's family. But she'd already met George and liked him; plus the heat would be off her, because everyone's attention would be on George and they'd all be trying their hardest to persuade him not to do anything reckless once he was out of plaster again. 'So am I going as your colleague who just happened to beat George at chess?' she asked carefully.

'Um, no. George has told them all that my new nickname's Tarzan. And why. And I can't even shake him for it because he claims he might still have concussion.'

Ed looked so disgusted that Jane couldn't help laughing. 'Poor George. He really is bored, isn't he? Of course I'll come.' She paused. 'Um, what do I wear?' Fashion had never been her strength. What did you wear when you met a baron? Was she going to have to grab Sorcha for an emergency clothes-shopping trip?

'Wear anything you like. It's the country pile, so I'd suggest something dogproof. If it helps, I'm wearing jeans.'

On Sunday morning, Ed drove them to his family home in Suffolk. It didn't take as long as Jane had expected before Ed turned into a long tree-lined drive. Finally, the house came into view and Ed parked on the gravel in front of it. The hall was a huge redbrick building with stone mullioned windows; at each corner there was a narrow tower, each capped with a leaded domed roof.

'Wow, it's gorgeous,' she said. 'And I take it that's the money-eating roof George was telling me about?'

'It certainly is,' Ed said with a rueful smile.

'Has your family lived here very long?' She grimaced. 'Sorry, I'm being nosey. I didn't look you up on the Internet because—well, it felt a bit too much like spying.'

'Ask whatever you like. And it's not spying.' Ed took her hand and squeezed it. 'Yes, the Somers family has lived here ever since the house was built, nearly five centuries ago. Dad's the fifteenth baron. There is a little bit of family money left, but back in Victorian times there was a baron who dabbled in scientific experiments and rather neglected everything else, and my great-grandfather lost a small fortune in the Wall Street Crash. So I guess we're like a lot of old families—land-rich and a bit cash-poor, because the maintenance is crippling and everything's entailed.'

'Meaning you can't sell because it has to go to the next generation?'

'Exactly. Dad says we're custodians and we're privileged to have grown up here. And he's right. We are.' He stole a kiss. 'We have a maze. I am *so* showing you that.'

'A maze. Like Hampton Court?' she asked.

'Sort of, but on a much smaller scale. And the rose garden. Dad's got a thing about roses. But it's fabulous—at this time of year, you walk through and you just breathe in the scent and it's like drinking roses.'

'So it's a big garden?'

He nodded. 'It's open to the public on Wednesdays and Saturdays, and whatever national garden open days Dad wants to do. The estate has to support itself. Frances got the hall licensed for weddings five years ago, so we can offer packages; and there's a minstrel's gallery in the Great Hall, so we sometimes hold concerts here.' He shrugged. 'Most summer weekends, there's something on; we're lucky that this weekend it's just us. Come on. Dad and Frances are expecting us.'

She followed him over to the front door, feeling ever so slightly out of her depth. As soon as Ed opened the front door, three dogs bounded down the hallway, barking madly and their tails a wagging blur. Jane crouched down to greet them and had her face thoroughly licked by the chocolate Labrador.

'That's Pepper,' he said. 'The Westie's called Wolfgang, and the setter's Hattie, short for "Hatter" because she's as mad as one.'

'They're lovely.' She continued making a fuss of them. How lucky Ed had been, growing up in a sprawling place like this. She'd just bet that the children had all been encouraged to run around the garden, with no shouting if they got grubby because it would all come out in the wash. Her own family had lived in a smart London apartment with too much glass and all-white furniture you didn't dare touch in case you left fingermarks. Which was fine for Jenna, who'd perfected elegance at a very early age, but Jane had always been in trouble for breaking things and making a mess. Even in her parents' new home in Cornwall, the furniture was so carefully arranged that the rooms felt ready for a photo shoot; you didn't dare relax in case you moved a cushion out of place.

'Ed, we're so glad you could make it.' A tall, elegant woman hugged him.

Jane got to her feet, aware that she was already covered in dog hair and slightly dishevelled. Not exactly the best impression she could make on Ed's family, but never mind.

'And you must be Jane. I'm Frances.' The older woman looked at her for a moment, as if considering shaking her hand, and Jane felt even more intimidated; and then she was enveloped in as huge a hug as Ed had received. 'It's so lovely to meet you. Come into the kitchen. It's a bit manic around here—but, then, George is home, so of course it's going to be manic.'

All her nervousness vanished instantly. Everything was going to be just fine. Ed's parents weren't in the slightest bit snobby; they were warm and welcoming, like Ed himself. As she followed Ed and Frances into the kitchen, Jane was shocked to realise that she already felt at home here—far more so than she did in her own parents' home. Here, she knew she'd be accepted exactly for who she was; and she didn't feel like a disappointment, the second-best child.

The man sitting at the table with the Sunday papers spread out before him looked up. Even before they were introduced, Jane could see that this was George and Ed's father; he had the same colouring and strong features.

Ed's father stood up and hugged him. 'Ed, my boy.' Jane received the same warm greeting. 'It's so nice to meet you, Jane. Welcome.'

'Um, shouldn't I be curtseying or something?' she asked.

'Good God, no!' David smiled at her. 'Don't even think of standing on ceremony. We're perfectly normal. Well, possibly except George, and you've already met him—and you're just as he described you.' He gave Ed a speaking look. 'At least *one* of our sons tells us things, Tarzan.'

'Oh, no—he's got you at it as well,' Ed groaned, but he was laughing. 'And may I remind you that one of your sons doesn't also spend his time narrowly avoiding avalanches or paragliding into cliffs? You can't have it both ways, Dad. Sensible and silent, or mad and gossipy. Your choice.'

'Oh, stop it, you two.' Frances flapped a tea towel at them, laughing. 'Jane, you've just come all the way from London, so you must be gasping for some coffee.'

'I'd love some, but I can see you're up to your eyes.' Jane gestured to the pile of broad beans that Frances had clearly been podding. 'Shall I make the coffee for everyone, or would you prefer me to help you with the beans?'

Frances gave her an approving smile. 'Making the coffee would be lovely. Thank you.'

'So where's George?' Ed asked.

'In the library, plotting,' David said. 'He's thinking about setting up some ghost walks for the winter. And just talk him out of this fireworks idea, would you? It terrifies me that he's going to take a course, get qualified and start blowing things up.'

'Since when does George listen to me?' Ed asked.

'You'd be surprised. And he's set up the chess board, Jane; he's desperate for that rematch with you.'

'So Ed told me.' She smiled back at him.

'Are the girls here yet?' Ed asked.

'Bea's got a meeting but she'll be down just after lunch. Alice is bringing Charlotte with her from the ivory tower,' Frances said. 'They'll be here any time now.'

Jane made the coffee, and Ed added milk and sugar to various cups. 'We'd better take one of these to George.'

'With a straw,' Frances added. 'He's not coping very well with losing his independence.'

'I did warn you he'd be a terrible patient,' Ed said dryly. 'If he gets too fed up, he can always stay at my place.'

'In your flat, he'd be too cooped up. At least

here he can limp around the garden with the dogs and mutter that he's never going paragliding again,' David said with a smile.

Ed ushered Jane through narrow corridors to the library—a light, airy room with more bookshelves than Jane had ever seen in her life, with several battered leather sofas scattered about, a grand piano and a huge, huge fireplace.

George was reclining on one of the sofas with a pair of crutches propped next to him, and a small table on his other side with a chessboard set out on it.

'Janey. Lovely to see you. Excuse me for not standing up; I hurt a bit, today. And, yes, Ed, I have done my physio today, before you ask.'

'I didn't say a word.' Ed spread his hands. 'I know better than to nag.'

Pepper had sneaked in beside them, and curled up on the sofa between George and his crutches.

And Jane was happy to curl up on one end of the other sofa next to Ed and play chess with George, with Hattie's head resting on her knee. This was the most perfect Sunday ever, she thought. In a place where she felt as if she belonged.

She beat George again, much to his chagrin; but before he could ask for another rematch, the library door burst open.

'Georgie-boy. You have—'

'—done my physio, yes, Alice.' He rolled his eyes. 'It's Sunday. That means no nagging, OK?'

'You wish,' Alice said with a grin.

Ed introduced his sisters to Jane. She liked them on sight; Alice was as brisk as she'd expected and Charlotte looked like a scatty academic, but Jane already knew not to be fooled by that.

'Lovely to meet you, Jane. George tells us you're a doctor, too,' Alice said. 'Please tell me Ed didn't tell you about the red-faced squeaky business.'

Jane smiled at her. 'No comment.'

George gave a crack of laughter. 'Well, he's right. You were red-faced and squeaky. You still are.'

'I might be eight years younger than you, Georgie-boy,' Alice said crisply, 'but I at least have the sense not to fly into a cliff.'

'Yes, m'lud,' George teased.

'Milady,' Alice corrected. 'Except I'm not a judge. Yet.'

Jane could see exactly why the paparazzi were scared of Alice. Though she also had a feeling that Alice had as big a heart as her brothers.

Lunch was in the dining room. The table was set with porcelain, solid silver cutlery and what looked like ancient Venetian glassware; Jane was terrified she'd drop something priceless and break it.

Ed moved his foot against hers so she glanced at him, then gave her a reassuring wink as if he understood what she was worrying about and wanted to put her at her ease.

The meal turned out to be full of laughter and noise and teasing—good-natured teasing, not the stuff with a nasty edge that she was used to from Jenna—and Jane was most definitely included as part of the family. The food was fantastic, too; Ed hadn't been exaggerating when he'd said that Frances was a great cook. 'Thank you. This is the best roast beef I've ever had,' she said, meaning it.

'It's from one of our farms. And all the vegetables are from our kitchen garden—I'm making a proper potager,' Frances said, 'before David takes up the whole of the garden with his roses.'

She and David shared an affectionate glance, and Jane realised that was another thing missing from her own childhood. Her father had always been tiptoeing round her mother, careful not to upset her, but there had never been that look of affection or adoration between them.

Alice was taking full advantage of the fact that George still couldn't manage cutlery and was making a big deal of spoon-feeding him.

'That's it—Frances, from now on I'm living on soup, custard, and anything else you can stick through a blender and I can drink through a straw,' George said with a pained look.

'No, you're not. This is such sweet revenge for all the times you spoon-fed me when I was a toddler and deliberately got yoghurt up my nose,' Alice said.

'Behave, children,' Frances said, laughing.

Alice gave George a hug. 'You can't get Mum to stick roast beef through a blender. It'd be disgusting. And you know I love you, really.'

'Love you, too, even though you're the bossiest woman I've ever met. Ruffle your hair for me, will you? I can't do it with these mitts. Not without cracking your skull, anyway,' he said wryly.

Jane was aware of a rush of envy as well as wistfulness. How wonderful it must've been, growing up in this kind of atmosphere, laughing and joking and secure in the knowledge that you were really, really loved.

After lunch, Ed took her for a stroll round the gardens. They were utterly beautiful and she could see why the public flocked there. The rose garden in particular was fantastic. 'Wow. You were right about the incredible scent,' she said, inhaling appreciatively.

'Do tell Dad. He'll be pleased. These are his babies, now we've all left home,' Ed said with a smile.

The promised maze was small, but big enough to be very private, and Ed kissed her at every corner before finally taking her back in to join the family.

Bea arrived mid-afternoon. 'Sorry I'm late. I'm up to my eyes in meetings, right now—but it's going to be *such* a good commission. I think it's going to be the one that'll make my name,' she said. And then she proceeded to grill Jane over coffee at the kitchen table, abetted by Alice and Charlotte.

'Charlotte, do you want me to fetch the spot-lamp from Dad's office so you can really make this an interrogation?' Ed asked in exasperation.

But Jane didn't mind at all. 'It's great that you look out for Ed.' She smiled at them. 'Anyway, my best friend did exactly the same thing to him, the first time she met him.'

'Don't you have any brothers and sisters to look out for you?' Alice asked.

'No.' Technically, she had a twin sister; but Jenna had never looked out for her. It had always been the other way round.

'Hmm. In that case, you can borrow us,' Charlotte said.

Looking at her, Jane realised that she meant it. And there was a huge lump in her throat as she hugged Ed's sisters.

'Your family's just *lovely*,' she said on the way back to London that evening.

'I know. And I told you they'd love you,' Ed said.

She could see the question on his face: when was she going to let him meet her family?

'Mine aren't like yours,' she said carefully. 'I'm not close to them.' She made regular duty phone calls home, but she hadn't actually seen her parents since Shaun had cheated on her with Jenna. And she most definitely hadn't seen her twin. She'd needed to take a step back and put some distance between them.

Ed reached across to squeeze her hand briefly. 'I can't imagine you not being close to anyone. My family loved you straight away.'

She dragged in a breath. 'You know I told you my mum was a model? Well, she didn't plan to have children. Pregnancy was hard for her.' Especially as she was carrying twins. Not that she could bring herself to tell Ed that, because then she knew he'd ask her about Jenna. 'She wasn't able to work during her pregnancy. Then she had really bad post-natal depression. And she couldn't go back to her career.'

'Why not?'

'Cover shoots and stretch marks don't mix,' she said dryly. It had been one of her mother's mantras. Though at least one of her daughters had been able to get her back into that charmed world. Going on photo shoots with Jenna had brought a small measure of happiness back to Sophia. Whereas Jane's world was alien to her. Disgusting. Particularly as it involved working with babies...the things that had ruined Sophia's life. She sighed. 'Appearances are really important to my mother. I'm never going to be tall, thin and elegant—and I'm clumsy. I drop things.'

'No, you don't.'

She coughed. 'If you remember, the very second I met you I spilled a whole glass of champagne over you.'

'Which wasn't your fault—someone knocked into you.' He paused. 'So your mother blames you for the end of her career?'

'If she hadn't been pregnant, she wouldn't have had stretch marks. Or had PND. She could've carried on doing what she loved.' Jane shrugged. 'And I can understand that. I know how I'd feel if I had to give up my job. It's who I am—just as modelling was who she was. She's fragile.'

'Fragile?'

'She has depression,' Jane said. 'On bad days, she doesn't get out of bed. Bad days can last for weeks. And, yes, she's seen doctors about it. Depression's tricky. It doesn't always respond to treatment.' She sighed. 'It's a matter of keeping her on as an even keel as we can. I guess seeing me upsets her, reminds her too much of what she's lost.'

Ed pulled off at the next layby.

'Ed? Why have we stopped?'

'Come here.' He pulled her into his arms. 'I'm sorry that your mum can't see you for who you are. And blaming you for losing her career—that's really not fair. You didn't ask to be born. What about your dad? Can't he help her see things differently?'

'He…' How could she put this? 'He's a bit like Mike Duffield. He likes a quiet life. Which is ironic, considering he used to be in advertising—that's how he met Mum. She was a model on one of his campaigns.'

Ed stroked her hair. 'I'm sorry. I wish I could fix this for you.'

'I don't think even a superhero could fix it. But it's fine. I'm used to it.'

The expression on his face said that he didn't think it was something you got used to. But he kissed the tip of her nose. 'Come on. Let's go home.'

CHAPTER ELEVEN

OVER the next couple of weeks, Ed and Jane grew closer still.

On the Friday night, Ed told Jane to dress up. 'A prom-type dress,' he said, 'seeing as you always ask me about dress codes. But I'm not telling you where we're going—it's a surprise.'

The first surprise was that he picked her up in a vintage sports car.

'It's George's. I'm taking full advantage,' Ed told her with a grin. 'He says he's going to inspect it minutely when I take it back on Sunday, and if there's a single speck of dust on it, I'm toast.'

She laughed. 'We'd better get a chamois leather and beat him to it.'

He opened the door for her and helped her inside.

It was the first time she'd ever sat in a low-slung sports car. 'Wow. I feel like a princess,' she said.

'Good. You look like one.'

'Thank you.' She felt colour seeping into her cheeks.

He stole a kiss. 'You're so sweet.'

'I haven't missed your birthday or anything, have I?' she asked.

'No. I just wanted to make you feel a bit special and have some fun.' He squeezed her hand, then drove her to a very swish hotel, handed the keys to the valet, and ushered her inside.

'Doesn't this place have three Michelin stars and you have to book up months in advance?' she asked.

'Yes to the first, usually to the second, but they had a last-minute cancellation. I had to book the tasting menu in advance. I hope that's OK?'

She smiled. 'That's more than OK. I've always wanted to do something like this. Ed, this is such a treat.'

'Good.' He looked pleased that she liked his surprise.

Ed stuck to mineral water because he was driving, but he ordered her a glass of champagne.

'One's definitely enough,' she said softly. She smiled at him. 'And I'll try not to spill this one over you.'

He laughed. 'Good. But I'm still taking you dancing, afterwards.' His eyes glittered. 'And I have plans after that.'

Repeating the night they'd first met. Except this time they really knew each other. A thrill of pure desire skittered through her. 'That,' she said, her voice husky, 'sounds just about perfect.'

The food was amazing; she savoured every mouthful.

And the dancing turned out to be very similar to that of the night of the hospital ball. Just like before, Ed made her feel as if she were floating when she danced with him.

'That was the perfect evening,' she said when he'd driven her home. 'Thank you. You made me feel really special.'

'That,' Ed told her, 'is because you are.'

And then he proceeded to show her exactly how.

At work, too, Jane found that she and Ed were completely in tune. When Pippa Duffield started bleeding in the shower and Iris came to fetch them from the patient they were seeing, they spoke in unison: 'We're going to need the anaesthetist and the neonatologist, and we need Pippa in Theatre now.'

Jane got one of the nurses to call Mike Duffield and put him on speaker phone for her while she scrubbed in. 'Mike, it's Jane Cooper from the hospital. Unfortunately, Pippa's started bleeding again, so we need to deliver the twins now.'

'Are they going to be all right?' he asked anxiously.

'I'm sure they will be,' Jane said, 'but the bad news is that we have to give Pippa a general anaesthetic, so you won't be able to come in with us and see the twins being born as we'd planned. But you can see them as soon as they've been checked over.'

'Tell Pip I love her,' Mike said, 'and I'm on my way now.'

Pippa was in tears. 'I didn't do anything out of the ordinary. I've been taking it so easy ever since I've been here. I can't understand why I started bleeding like that. And there was so much of it!'

'I know, and it's not your fault,' Jane soothed. 'We did say this might happen, and you're in exactly the right place for us to help you.'

'Two days before the babies were going to be delivered anyway. Why couldn't I have hung on for just two more days?' Pippa asked despairingly.

'That's just the way it goes sometimes,' Ed told her gently. 'Pippa, there's something else we need to talk about. If we can't stop the bleeding, we might have to give you a hysterectomy. We'll only do that if there's no other way, but may we have your consent?'

'So…then I won't ever be able to have another baby? Even with IVF?'

'No,' he confirmed quietly. 'I know this is a lot to take in, and it's unfair of us to dump this on you right now when you're worried sick about the babies, but we do have to think about you as well.'

Pippa swallowed hard. 'And if I don't have a

hysterectomy, would that mean you can't stop the bleeding and I'll…?'

Jane squeezed her hand, realising that Pippa knew exactly what the consequences were but just couldn't say it. If they couldn't stop the bleeding, she would die. 'Yes.'

Pippa dragged in a breath. 'If it's the only way, then do what you have to. Just make sure the babies are safe.'

'Thank you,' Ed said.

She bit her lip. 'I so wanted Mike to cut the cords.'

'I know,' Jane said.

'Nothing's gone to plan.'

'But the babies will be here safely soon, and Mike's on his way. He told me to tell you that he loves you,' Jane said, and held Pippa's hand while the anaesthetist counted her down.

In Theatre, Ed swiftly made the incision; he delivered the first twin into Iris's waiting hands, ready to be wrapped in a towel and checked over by the neonatologist.

Just after he'd delivered the second twin, the

anaesthetist said, 'Blood pressure's still dropping.'

Just what they'd wanted to avoid: Pippa was haemorrhaging.

Although they were prepared for it and had ordered cross-matched blood, the transfusion didn't seem to be helping. Jane went cold. Please don't let Pippa go into DIC. Disseminated intravascular coagulation meant that the clotting factors in the blood were activated throughout the body instead of being localised to the site of the injury, so small blood clots developed through the body, using up the blood's clotting factors so it couldn't clot where it was really needed.

If they couldn't get her blood to start clotting, there was a very good chance they were going to lose her, and she'd never get to meet the twin girls she'd wanted so desperately.

They continued pumping blood into her.

Please, please, let her start clotting, Jane prayed silently.

After what felt like a lifetime, the anaesthetist said softly, 'We're there. Blood pressure rising nicely.'

'Thank God,' Ed said softly.

Finally they managed to close the incision ready to take Pippa through to the recovery room.

'How are the babies doing?' Ed asked.

'I'm going to take them to the special care unit for a while; I want them on oxygen for a bit. But they're fighters, like their mum. They'll be fine,' the neonatologist said.

'We need to take pictures of the babies for her, for when she wakes up,' Jane said.

Iris grabbed the camera they kept for this kind of situation and took pictures of the twins. While Ed sat with Jane as she started to wake up, Jane went out into the corridor. Mike was there, pacing.

'What's happened?' he asked desperately.

'You have two beautiful girls, and Pippa's waking up now,' she said, smiling.

'Can I see them?' he asked.

'The babies are going down to Special Care—not because there's a major problem but at this age they often need a little bit of help breathing.' There would be time enough to let him know that they'd been close to losing Pippa; for now, she wanted him to enjoy the first few minutes of being a dad.

She took him through to the recovery room; he held Pippa tightly. 'I was so worried.'

'I'm fine. But the babies…they're in the special care unit.' A tear trickled down her face.

'We've taken pictures for you for now, until you're ready to go and see them,' Iris said, and handed over the photographs.

Mike and Pippa were both crying. 'They're so tiny.'

'They're good weights for thirty-five weeks,' Ed said. 'I know it's easy for me to say, but try not to worry. They're doing just fine.'

Back at Jane's flat that night, they collapsed into bed.

'What a day,' Jane said.

'Mmm. I had a few bad moments,' Ed admitted. 'If she'd gone into DIC…'

'But she didn't. It was a good outcome. Twin girls, both doing well, and with luck they'll be out of Special Care within the week.'

'We did well today,' he said with a smile. 'Great teamwork.'

'Absolutely.' Jane curled into his arms. Funny, she'd never thought she could ever be this happy. Neither of them had actually declared their feelings, but she knew. She'd fallen in love with Ed, and she was pretty sure that Ed loved her all the way back. Just the way she was.

Life couldn't get any better than this. She just hoped it could stay this way.

The next morning, Jane called in to see how Pippa was doing, to find her in floods of tears.

'I'm just so tired—and I'm dreading Mike's mum coming in to see the babies and taking over,' Pippa confessed.

Jane sat next to her and took her hands. 'You've been through an awful lot, Pip. And, the thing is, Mike's mum doesn't know the half of it. I reckon if you tell her what's been happening, she'll be a lot gentler with you than you expect. She'll realise that you need support and help, not someone taking over and telling you what to do.

'But we've never been close. She always made it clear she felt I took her son away.'

'Maybe,' Jane said softly, 'that's a defence mechanism. Mike's her only child, is he?'

Pippa nodded.

'Maybe she always wanted a daughter as well— and, now she's got one, she's scared she's going to get it wrong because she's used to just having a son, and she's too proud to tell you. Just like you're too proud to tell her that you went through IVF,' Jane said, 'Right now, I think you could do with a mum to lean on, so why don't you talk to her? Tell her how you feel.'

Pippa bit her lip. 'It's hard.'

'But it'll be worth it if it lets you build that bridge.'

'Do you think so?'

'I know so,' Jane said confidently.

Later that afternoon, she dropped in to see Pippa again, and was surprised to see an older woman sitting on the side of the bed, cuddling one of the twins and talking animatedly to Pippa.

'Jane, this is my mother-in-law,' Pippa said, introducing them almost shyly.

'Pip's told me so much about you,' Mrs Duffield said. 'She says you've been so supportive, right from the moment she had the pregnancy test after her IVF.'

So Pippa had taken her advice, Jane thought. And clearly that bridge had been built from the other side, too. She smiled. 'That's what I'm here for. And it's lovely to see the babies getting stronger and stronger every day.'

Mrs Duffield beamed. 'I'm so looking forward to being a hands-on granny. But things have changed a lot since my day, so I'm taking my lead from Pip.'

Jane looked at Pippa, who mouthed, 'Thank you. You were absolutely right.'

Jane had to blink back the tears. 'Well, if there's anything you need, any questions you have, just ask. And congratulations on being a granny of twins.'

'They're beautiful. Just like their mother,' Mrs Duffield said. 'Though I think they both have Mike's smile.'

'Yeah.' If only she could find a way to build a bridge like this with her own mother, Jane thought. But she pushed it aside. Brooding wasn't going to help anyone. 'I'll see you later,' she said with a smile.

CHAPTER TWELVE

A COUPLE of weeks later, Ed dropped in at his
brother's flat on his way home.

'How are you managing, now the plaster's off?'
he asked.

'Fine.' But George's smile didn't reach his eyes.

'What's up?'

George sighed. 'Nothing.'

'Come off it. Fed up with being stuck in the
slow lane?'

'I guess.' George shrugged.

'OK. Let's take your car,' Ed suggested. 'I'm
not breaking the speed limit for you, but a quick
drive up the motorway with the top down might
make you feel a bit better.'

George dragged in a breath. 'Sometimes I wish
you weren't so nice. It'd be easier.'

'What would?'

'Nothing.'

Ed took his brother's hands. 'Is this about the fertility stuff? Look, they said it takes time. Don't write yourself off just yet. You took a hard knock when you hit the cliff. Wait until the next test. And even if the motility of your sperm doesn't get much better than it is now, it doesn't mean you can't ever have kids. There's a special form of IVF called ICSI that could work for you—they pick out the best sperm and use them.'

'It's not that.' George looked bleak. 'Forget it.'

'No. George, I can see that something's wrong.' He'd been sure of it when George had been in hospital, too. 'You're my brother. You've always been there for me. Let me be there for you.'

George's face was full of anguish. 'What if I'm not your brother?'

Ed frowned. 'Of course you're my brother.'

'I might not be.'

'How do you work that out? We have the same parents.'

'Not necessarily. Supposing Dad isn't my father?'

'Of course he is.' Ed frowned, too. 'George, you and I look alike. We've got the same colouring, the same cleft in our chin—exactly the same as Dad's.'

'We're not *that* alike,' George said.

'Where's this all coming from?' Ed asked, mystified.

'I've read her diaries.'

Ed didn't have to ask whose. Because something was becoming nastily clear. He'd been right about the unfinished business. 'Is that the package you had to collect from the solicitor's, earlier this year?' The meeting that only George had been invited to after their mother's death; Ed had pushed aside the hurt at the time. Of course it would be George. He was the eldest of her two children.

'Her diaries, letters and photographs.' George gave a mirthless laugh. 'I knew Dad used to send her photographs of us on our birthday. Stupidly, I thought she might've kept them. She didn't—the photos were of the men in her life. But I started reading the letters and the diaries.' He shook his head. 'I really don't know how to tell Dad. Ed, I know it for sure. I'm not his.'

'But *how* do you know?'

'She had an affair. Well, more than one, while she was married to Dad. And…Dad just isn't my biological father.'

'No way. You look like Dad. You look like me,' Ed said again.

'Maybe the guy looked a bit like Dad—maybe he had the same colouring and build and what have you.' George blew out a breath. 'I hate to think the girls aren't really my sisters.'

'They're your sisters, all right. The same as I'm your brother. Nothing's going to change that.' Ed paused. 'Is this why you've been taking more risks than usual, the last few months? Since you first read her papers and came to that completely crazy conclusion?'

'It's not crazy. It's the truth.' George sighed. 'Yes.'

'And this was what was distracting you when you crashed?'

George nodded.

'And you've kept this to yourself for months? You *idiot*. Why didn't you tell me?'

'Apart from the fact that you were in beating yourself up over your divorce and I didn't want to dump yet more burdens on you, I guess I didn't know how. And I kept hoping that maybe I'd got the wrong end of the stick. When I woke up after the crash, I thought maybe I'd got it all wrong and I was being an idiot. But I've read the diaries again, since I've been back home. And the letters.' He limped over to the dresser, pulled out a thick envelope, rummaged through it and brought out a diary and a handful of letters. He dumped them on Ed's lap. 'Read them and tell me if I've got it wrong.'

He'd marked the pages with a sticky note. Ed read through them, and went cold.

'She doesn't say you're definitely not Dad's. She says she's not sure.'

'Which is the same thing.'

'No, it's not. Look, we can do a DNA test. That'll prove it for sure.'

'But what if,' George whispered, 'what if a DNA test proves I'm not who I always thought I am?'

Ed could see the demons haunting his brother. He was afraid of being the cuckoo in the nest, unwanted by their family. Just as they'd both been unwanted by their mother. 'It won't matter at all,' he said softly. 'I don't give a damn about genetics. You're my brother and I love you. I know the girls will feel the same. And Dad and Frances.'

'Maybe.'

'No, *definitely*. You're ours, and you always will be.' He gave George a hug. 'I love you.'

'And I love you, too.' George looked bleak as Ed put the papers on the table and came back to sit beside him. 'But if I'm not Dad's, that means legally we're talking about a whole new kettle of fish. It means I'm not the heir. *You* are, Ed,' he said softly.

Ed was glad he was sitting down. If he was the heir… It meant he'd have to give up the job he loved to run the estate. He couldn't be selfish; he'd have to put his duty first. Of course he'd do it.

But this didn't just impact on him. How would Jane react to the idea of such a change in his life—and what it would mean for her, if their future was together?

'Oh, hell,' Ed said.

'You get it now?' George asked dryly.

'I get it.' Ed ran a hand through his hair. 'So how are we going to deal with this?'

'I don't know. I've got to think of a way of breaking it to Dad. Without hurting him.'

'We need to do the DNA test first.'

'Right, and I can really say to him that I need a sample of his DNA for a quick paternity test. Not.' George rolled his eyes.

'Maybe they can test you and me, to see if we have parents in common.'

'And what if we both have different fathers, and neither of them's Dad? Or if we do have the same father, and he isn't Dad?'

Ed hadn't thought about that. 'This is one hell of a mess.'

'You're telling me.' George swallowed hard. 'All these years, I've tried to tell myself that it doesn't matter. That I have Dad and Frances and you and the girls, and it doesn't matter that she left us. I tried to feel sorry for her, because I knew she was unhappy. But now…' He shook his head and grimaced. 'I just wish I'd never seen those bloody papers.'

'So do I,' Ed said. 'Not just for me, but because you've been going through hell ever since you read them. I hate to think you've been brooding when I could've been there for you. I *knew* there was something wrong. I even asked you about it. And you still didn't tell me.'

'You know what they say about a problem shared being a problem halved? It's completely untrue. I just told you and it's double the misery.' George looked bleak. 'I have no idea how we're going to sort this.'

'We need DNA testing. You, me and Dad. There isn't any other way.' Ed thought about it. 'I know people in the lab at work, but they don't do DNA testing. We'll need a specialist lab. Maybe Alice knows a reliable, discreet one?'

'I don't want Alice involved,' George said immediately.

'Then we're going to have to tell Dad and get the test done. There's no other way round it, George.'

'How long does testing take?' George asked.

'I have no idea. And it'll depend on the workload of the lab as well as the physical time it takes for the test to run,' Ed warned.

'This feels like all the exams I've ever taken, rolled into one,' George said. 'Except this time I don't have a clue what the results are going to be. And I don't know if I'm going to pass.'

'Whatever the results say, you're my brother and that's never going to change. Dad, Frances and the girls won't stop loving you, either.'

'Damn, I'm so bloody wet,' George said, closing his eyes and rubbing his forehead.

'No, I'd feel the same.' Ed gave him a wry smile. 'Actually, now I think about it, it's the same for me, too. How do I know that Dad's my biological father? And if he's not...then who the hell am I?'

'This weekend,' George said, 'is going to be one of the worst of my life. And yours.' He limped over to the table to collect his laptop. 'Right. Let's find ourselves a lab.'

'You start looking them and I'll make us some coffee,' Ed said. 'We'll sort this out. Together.'

'Yeah.' George gave a deep sigh. 'Thanks.'

'Well, what did you think I was going to do?

Make you the worst breakfast in the universe and make you drink tea with too much sugar in it?'

'It worked for you,' George said. 'But please don't do it to me. Coffee's fine.'

Ed laughed, then sobered slightly. 'I know we're keeping this quiet for now, but I do need to let Jane know what's going on.'

'Because it's going to affect her as well. If it gets messy, she'll end up under the spotlight because she's your girl,' George said.

'She won't leak it.'

George rolled his eyes. 'State the obvious, why don't you?'

'Yeah.' Ed was heartened that his brother could see it, too.

In the kitchen, he texted Jane swiftly. *Running a bit late. Don't wait dinner for me. Still OK to call in later?*

Her reply was almost instant. *Course it is. Is everything OK? George?* she texted.

I'll explain later, Ed replied. *Don't worry.*

Though not worrying was a lot easier said than done.

* * *

When Ed left George's flat, he headed straight for Jane's flat.

'You look like hell,' Jane said when she opened the door, and wrapped her arms round him.

He leaned his cheek against her hair, breathing in the comforting, familiar scent of her shampoo. 'Sometimes life really sucks.'

She shepherded him inside. 'Come and sit down. Have you eaten?'

'I'm not hungry. But I wouldn't say no to a mug of tea with about ten sugars in it.'

'That bad?' She stroked his face. 'Tell me about it.'

'It's a long and very messy story,' he warned.

'I'm not going anywhere. And whatever you tell me won't go any further than me.'

'I know that.' He trusted her. He knew she wouldn't lie to him.

He let her lead him into the kitchen and sat down. When she'd switched the kettle on, he scooped her onto his lap. Just holding her made things feel a bit better.

'So what's happened?' she asked softly.

He sighed. 'You know Frances is my step-mother.'

She nodded.

'My biological mother left Dad for someone else when I was four and George was six. She never said goodbye, and she never sent either of us so much as a Christmas card or a birthday card after she left.' The fact that she hadn't wanted them: Ed was pretty sure it was half the reason why George wouldn't settle down with anyone. His brother didn't want to risk being abandoned again.

He'd made that mistake himself, with Camilla. He'd thought he was doing the right thing by her. That together they'd make a family, a strong one like his father and Frances had. But when he'd turned out to be completely wrong and Camilla had left, it had brought back some of the old hurt, the stuff he'd thought buried and forgotten about.

He sighed. 'I know Dad would never have done anything underhand like not giving us her cards. George said he used to send her photographs of us every Christmas, trying to build bridges that she just knocked down every time. And I once overheard him ranting about her to my godfather. He said he could forgive her for leaving him, but he couldn't forgive her for how she'd behaved to me and George.'

'Oh, Ed. How could she possibly...?' She swallowed hard. 'I just can't imagine walking away from my children. Not that I have any, obviously, but... How could she do it?'

'Because she was damaged,' Ed said softly. 'Dad's love wasn't enough for her. Her children weren't enough for her. And all the men she flitted between—they were never enough for her, either. Sometimes I think that maybe she did love us really—that she realised Dad would be able to give us a happy, loving childhood more than she could, and she stayed away because she didn't want to wreck that.'

And now for the biggie. 'George thinks he's not Dad's.'

'Why?'

'She died earlier this year, and her solicitor gave George her diaries and some old letters. He read them, and he's convinced himself that all the evidence says he isn't Dad's.'

'Could he be right?'

Ed sighed. 'I don't know. But that's why he's been so reckless, these last few months. He was thinking about it when he had the accident. And he's been brooding about it ever since.'

'Poor George. But he does have you.'

'That's what I told him.' Ed sighed again. The only way to be sure of the truth is to take a DNA test. We're telling Dad this weekend and taking the test kits with us.'

'What can I do to help?'

He'd known Jane would say that. She had the biggest heart of anyone he'd met. He held her tighter. 'Nothing.'

'Even if all I can do is listen or give you a bit of moral support, I want you to know I'm here.' She kissed him lightly. 'Anything you want me to do, just say. If you want me there with you at the weekend, that's fine. Though it's pretty sensitive. So if you'd rather leave it as just you, your dad and George, that's also fine—I won't go huffy on you.'

'Thank you.' He gave a tired smile. 'I have to be honest with you. I don't have a clue what's going to happen next. If the test proves that George and I really are Dad's, then that's brilliant and we can stop worrying. But we have to be prepared for it not to go our way. If we're *not* Dad's, then the papers are going to drag up some truly horrible stuff. Things about my mother flitting from man to man, things about George never dating anyone more than three times because he's a chip off the old block.' He paused. 'I hate to think of you being dragged through what could end up being a real mess. So if you'd rather walk away now, I understand.'

She shook her head. 'No chance. I don't care what the papers say and I don't care what the DNA test says. I know *you*, and that's all that matters.'

She was standing by him. Regardless. Ed's chest felt tight. 'Thank you. But if you do change your mind, then I'll understand that, too.'

'I'm not going to change my mind.' Jane held his gaze. 'I'm not Camilla. Just as you're not Shaun.'

Camilla might have sat it out until the DNA test results came through, especially if there was a chance that Ed could be the heir to the barony. But if the tests had shown him not to be David Somers's son, he knew how she would've reacted. The complete opposite from Jane.

And there was a subject he'd been avoiding. Since they were talking about difficult stuff already, they might as well add this to the whole mess, he thought. 'I know George told you about the baby. And he probably told you his theory.'

'That she lied to you about being pregnant in the first place.' She nodded. 'Is he right?'

Ed shrugged. 'Maybe. But you know as well as I do how many pregnancies end up in an early miscarriage. And, once you're in the middle of wedding preparations, it's not that easy to say you've changed your mind and call a halt to everything. Especially when it's a society wedding and there'd be so much talk.'

She could understand that; and for Ed to give his ex the benefit of the doubt like that just showed what a huge heart he had. 'Did Camilla know about your mum?'

'Her family have known mine for years.' He

shrugged. 'I guess they must have talked about it at some point.'

'So she knew you wouldn't walk away from her if she was accidentally pregnant,' Jane said softly. 'Because you're a good man and you do what's right.'

'I tried. But I wasn't what she really wanted. And I *was* selfish, Janey. It wasn't all her fault. I didn't give her the choice about moving to Glasgow,' he reminded her.

'She didn't give you a choice about getting married,' Jane pointed out. 'Or about the baby.' She paused. 'I'm not going to ask you if you wanted a family. I've seen you with your sisters, and I've seen you with the babies on the ward. You never miss a chance to chat to a mum and cuddle a baby.'

'Busted,' Ed said with a wry smile. 'Yes. I wanted a family. But later, when I suggested we try again, she made it clear that the baby had been a mistake and she didn't want to try again.'

Jane swallowed. 'You don't think she…?'

'Had a termination?' He shook his head. 'She wasn't that hard-bitten.' He stole a kiss. 'I've seen you with the babies on the ward too, Dr Cooper. Is that what you wanted with Shaun?'

'A family. Like the one I didn't grow up in,' she said. 'But I don't think that was what he wanted.'

'More fool him.' Ed stole another kiss. 'Jane—I know we only met a couple of months ago. It's probably way too soon for me to say anything. And I shouldn't be saying anything at all when my family's in such a mess. But I know how I feel about you, and I just…' He swallowed hard. 'I love you. Ever since I've met you, I've felt so in tune with you. I told myself I'd be sensible and I wouldn't repeat my mistakes with Camilla, that I wouldn't let anyone get close to me again. But I can't help myself; with you, I feel complete.'

'Oh, Ed.' Her eyes filled with tears. 'I…I never thought I'd let myself feel like that about anyone, either. That I'd learn to trust again. But you—you're different. And I love you, too.'

'Thank God,' Ed whispered, and kissed her.

CHAPTER THIRTEEN

On Saturday morning, Ed felt as if he was driving the condemned man to the gallows—except George might not be the only one who was condemned.

He half wished he'd asked Jane to come with him. Her calm, quiet support would have helped. Then again, given the bombshell that he and George were about to drop on their father, maybe it did need to be just the three of them and Frances.

He drove on through the rain with a heavy heart.

Jane reached for the entryphone. Had Ed changed his mind and wanted her to go with him to Suffolk after all? 'Hello?'

'It's me.'

Jenna. Jane recognised the voice instantly, and

ice slid down her spine. What did her twin want? Given the radio silence since that article had hit the news stands, she guessed it wouldn't be to apologise.

'Are you going to let me in, or what?' Jenna asked. 'It's peeing down out here and my hair's getting wet.'

For a moment, Jane wondered what would happen if she said no. Then she remembered what she'd said to Pippa Duffield about building bridges. It had worked for Pippa. Maybe this time it would work for her. 'Come up,' she said, suppressing a sigh and pressing the button to let Jenna in through the building's front door.

The kettle had boiled and Jane was infusing peppermint tea by the time there was a knock on the door.

Jenna looked cross. 'You kept me waiting for *ages*.'

Oh, great. It looked as if her twin was spoiling for a fight. Jane tried to defuse the atmosphere. 'I made you some peppermint tea.' She didn't drink it herself, but she knew Jenna did, and she kept a stock in for her sister. 'I'll put some honey in the cup in a second.' She nodded at Jenna's luggage. 'Have you just come back from a shoot?'

Jenna rolled her eyes. 'Why else do you think I'm here?'

To get a convenient bed for the night. Not to see how her twin was and spend some quality time together. Jane suppressed the hurt. 'Where was the shoot?'

'The Big Apple.'

'A night flight home, then. You must be tired.' Jane tried to be conciliatory. 'Can I get you a late breakfast or something?'

Jenna rolled her eyes again. 'Little Dr Perfect.'

What? Jane frowned. 'What's this all about, Jenna?' OK, she could understand that her twin was tired and grumpy after travelling, but why did Jenna have to take it out on her?

'You always have to *nag*, don't you?'

Normally, Jane let it go and tried to avoid a full-on fight. But today she was keyed up, worried about Ed, and the question just burst out. 'Why do you hate me so much?'

'Why do you think? You and your perfect job

and your perfect life.' Jenna scowled at her. 'You have no idea what it's like to struggle.'

Jane couldn't believe she was hearing this, from Jenna of all people. Her childhood had been a lot tougher than Jenna's. The only time she'd ever really felt loved had been at Great-Aunt Sadie's. 'That's unfair. I've always tried to look after you. When we were kids and Mum was too ill, I used to cook dinner for us.'

'Exactly. Dr Perfect,' Jenna sneered. 'Always doing everything right. So *perfect*.'

'Perfect? Give me strength. You made my life a misery all the way through school. You and your friends laughed at me because I'm clumsy and I was always picked last for sports. You sneered because I studied instead of partying, and you made sure the whole school called me that horrible name.'

'Oh, you *studied*.' Jenna made exaggerated quote marks with her fingers. 'And don't we all know that you always got straight As? You're the clever one. I had it rammed down my throat all the time by the teachers—why couldn't I be more like you? The good twin, not the bad one.'

Said the girl who'd made her feel bad for not being like her. And now she was complaining? Jane saw red. 'If you'd made the slightest bit of effort in class instead of spending all your time fiddling with your hair and make-up, you could've done well in your exams, so don't you dare throw that at me. You made your choices and I accept that, so why do you have a problem that my choices were different? Why can't you just accept that we're different? I don't whine all the time that I'm not as tall and skinny as you. I accept myself for who I am. Why can't you do that?'

Jenna curled her lip. 'You're just jealous because I take after Mum.'

'No. I'm fine with who I am. But I'm tired of you putting me down all the time. Like having that horrible article printed.'

'It's not my fault the journo wrote it up like that.'

Jane doubted that. Jenna's publicist would've insisted on approving the copy.

'It's not just the article, it's been my entire life. Even my first boyfriend—I'd had a crush on him for months and I could hardly believe he wanted to go out with me. The day after our date, it was all round the school that he'd lost a bet with you and his forfeit was to date me. That's the only reason he asked me out.'

Jenna shrugged. 'It never seemed to bother you.'

No, because Jane had been determined not to let Jenna see how much it hurt. Or how it had felt when she'd discovered during her teens that half of her boyfriends were only dating her in the hope they'd meet Jenna, and the other half saw what they were missing as soon as they met her twin and dumped her. Before Ed, she'd had lousy taste in men.

'And Shaun.' Jenna had never apologised for that. 'I could've understood it if you'd fallen for him, if you really loved him—but you dumped him as soon as I left him.'

Jenna shrugged again. 'I didn't want him. It wasn't my fault. He came on to me.'

Jane had no idea if Jenna was telling the truth or twisting it. 'Couldn't you have said no?'

'He wasn't right for you—so, really, I did you

a favour. If you'd bought a flat together or even got married, it would've been harder for you to walk away, with all the legal mess and expense.'

Jane blinked. 'You slept with *my* fiancé, in *my* bed, and you're telling me you did me a *favour*?'

Jenna lifted her chin. 'You know I did.'

'What kind of weird planet do you live on?' Jane shook her head. She'd had enough. 'Jenna, I've tried and tried and tried to be a good sister to you. But I just can't do this any more. I'm tired of you pulling me down all the time and making me feel bad when I've done nothing wrong. I'm sure you have plenty of other people you can stay with in London. I'm going out now, and I'd prefer you not to be here when I get back.' Jane grabbed her coat and bag, and walked out of the flat before she said anything she'd *really* regret.

Jenna stared after her twin, absolutely furious. Little Doctor Perfect was throwing her out?

She wasn't in the mood for dragging down to Cornwall to stay with the parents. And now it looked as if she was going to have to find somewhere to stay.

She used Jane's landline to ring round her friends. Half of them were away on shoots, but she finally found someone who could put her up for the night. She was about to leave when the phone rang and the answering machine clicked in.

'Janey, it's Ed. I said I'd ring you when I got to the Hall. You're obviously out. I wish I was with you instead of here in Suffolk.' There was a sigh. 'George and I are going to talk to Dad about the paternity test stuff now. I'll ring you later, OK?' A pause. 'I love you.' And then the beep as he ended the message.

I love you? Jenna frowned. As far as she knew, Jane wasn't even seeing anyone. Who was this Ed person? Whoever he was, he lived in Suffolk, he'd gone to some hall or other, and there was someone called George.

Intrigued, she flicked into the search engine on her mobile phone and typed in *Ed, Suffolk, Hall, George*. Just to see what would come up.

Right at the top of the list there was a link to 'Visitor Information, Somers Hall'.

Jenna skimmed through it. Interesting. David

Somers, fifteenth baron, and his sons Edward and George. Hmm. It looked as if Jane was dating the younger son of a baron.

But why would Ed Somers be talking to his father about a paternity test?

Jenna thought about it a bit more, then smiled. Her contact at *Celebrity Life* would just *love* this story. And it would serve Jane right for being such a bitch and refusing to give her a bed for the night.

'What's all this about, Ed? You both look as if you haven't slept in days.' David frowned.

'You need to sit down, Dad. And you're going to need tea with about ten sugars,' Ed said.

'You're both here, so it's not as if George has finally managed to break his neck,' David said. 'What else could be that bad?'

'This.' George tossed the packet of letters and the diary onto the kitchen table. 'And I'm sorry, Dad, there's no way of softening it.'

'That's your mother's handwriting,' David said as he saw the open diary.

'Tea with ten sugars coming up,' Frances said with a sigh.

George told his father what he and Ed had worked out.

David looked in shock by the time George finished. 'I knew about the affairs, but it never occurred to me that you might be another man's child. Either of you.' His eyes narrowed. 'This doesn't change anything, you know. You're *mine*. Both of you.'

'And mine,' Frances chipped in. 'I know I'm not your biological mother, but you've both been my sons for more than a quarter of a century. I hope you two haven't been worrying about that.'

George and Ed exchanged a guilty glance.

'Idiots, the pair of you,' David said, rolling his eyes.

'Dad, there's the legal side to consider,' George said. 'I'm sorry, this is going to sound horrible and I'm certainly not wishing your life away, but we have to face it. If neither of us is yours, then the hall, the title and everything else reverts to another branch of the family when you die. Which means Frances loses her home and we

all lose our childhood. Given this evidence...'
He gestured to the papers.

'Which is all circumstantial, as Alice will no
doubt tell you,' David cut in.

'No. It sheds enough doubt on the matter to
mean that we need to do a DNA test,' Ed said
gently. 'We've found a lab.'

'And paid for the kits. They came to my place
yesterday,' George added.

'All you do is swab the inside of your mouth so
you get cells and saliva, let it dry out, send the
samples off in labelled envelopes and their ma-
chines do the rest,' Ed explained.

David sighed. 'Right. Let's get it over with.'

'We can't eat or drink for half an hour beforehand,' Ed said.

'Then tea is on hold,' Frances said, removing
the pot from the middle of the table.

'There's a set procedure to follow,' Ed continued. 'We need to use gloves to make sure that
none of the samples are contaminated, and the
samples all have to dry out in separate glasses.'

'This is where it's really useful to have a scientist in the family,' George said, patting Ed's shoulder.

'How long does it take before we get the results?' David asked.

'About five working days. So that means we have a week to wait,' Ed said. 'And, no, they can't do it any faster. George already asked.'

'Whatever the results, *nothing* is going to change the fact that you're my sons and I love you,' David said softly.

'I love you, too,' George and Ed echoed.

Ed left George in Suffolk, knowing that his brother could get a lift back to London with one of their sisters the next day, and drove back to London late that afternoon. Back at his flat, he rang Jane. 'I'm home.'

'How was it?' she asked.

He sighed. 'Difficult.'

'Do you want me to come over? Or do you want to come here?'

'Can I come to you? I could do with your warmth.' And his flat didn't feel like home, the way hers did.

'Come over now,' she said. 'I've been baking. The choc-chip cookies are fresh out of the oven.'

'Now there's an offer I can't refuse.' He smiled despite himself. 'See you in a bit.'

She buzzed him up as soon as he rang the entryphone. He took the stairs three at a time, and wrapped his arms round her. 'That's better,' he said softly.

'How are George and your dad bearing up?' she asked.

We're a united front,' he said. 'In private as well as in public. Dad says that whatever the results show, he doesn't give a damn about the barony or the hall. We're his, and nothing's going to change that. Frances said the same.'

'And so will your sisters. I could've told you that,' she said. 'It's so obvious in your family, the love and affection—the way you talk to each other, the way you look at each other.' She swallowed hard. 'A million miles away from the way my family is.'

He held her closer. 'Oh, Janey. I'm sorry they give you such a hard time.'

'Some things you can't fix, and you have to

learn not to beat yourself up about it,' she said. 'Remember that. And love…love can fix an awful lot of things. I'm not giving up on them quite yet.'

Monday morning started in a rush, with a breech birth where they needed to try turning the baby into a better position for delivery; and then a patient with all the symptoms of pre-eclampsia but with the addition of jaundice, meaning that it was more likely to be acute fatty liver of pregnancy. The only treatment was to deliver the baby; though, at thirty-five weeks, it was better for the baby to stay where he was for a while longer, until his lungs had matured properly.

Although the mum was on a drip to maintain her glucose levels and stop hypoglycaemia, routine monitoring of the baby showed that the foetus was in distress, and they ended up needing to take her straight into Theatre for an emergency section.

'We can't risk an epidural in case there's a bleed at the anaesthesia site. It'll have to be a general anaesthetic,' Ed said grimly.

Luckily the delivery was fine, without the mum

having any of the clotting problems Jane and Ed had worried about. And he caught her eye at the end of the operation, mouthing, 'Well done.'

They worked so well as a team. So in tune.

Jane was writing up the notes at her desk when the phone rang.

'Janey? It's Sorcha. I've just seen the papers on the ward and it's not good. There's a story about Ed and his family. About how there's a paternity test going on.'

Jane went cold. How could the press possibly have got hold of the story?

'And it's worse than that, Jane. The source—they say it's close to Ed Somers. His girlfriend.'

'No. That's not true. I don't understand.' Jane blew out a breath. 'Thanks for the heads-up, Sorcha. I'd better take a look online and find out just what they're saying.'

The story was all over the place. *Somers: who's the real heir?*

Oh, hell. She needed to talk to Ed. Right now.

He was in his own office, talking on the phone; he acknowledged her with a gesture, then finished his conversation and replaced the receiver.

'Ed, do you have minute? There's something you really need to see,' she said urgently.

He looked grim. 'If it's what I think you're going to say, I already know the story's leaked. George just called me. He's been trying to get hold of me all morning, except we were in Theatre.'

'I haven't talked to anyone about this, Ed. Nobody at all. But the one I read—' she felt sick '—it says the source is me.'

'Maybe someone overheard you talking to me about it.'

She shook her head. 'I don't see how. And if they had, then surely they would've said that you were the source, not me.' Then a seriously nasty thought hit her. 'Your phone message.' She closed her eyes. 'Oh, my God. Saturday, when you and George went to see your dad. When you called me and left a message. Jenna must've still been in my flat. On her own.'

He looked mystified. 'Who's Jenna?'

Her throat felt dry. 'Oh, God. Can I close your door?'

'Sure.' He looked concerned.

She did so, and sat on the edge of his desk. 'I'm

sorry, Ed. I should've told you about her before. You know I said my mum couldn't model any more once she was pregnant? It's because she was having twins.'

'You have a *twin*?' Ed looked at her in seeming disbelief. 'But you said you were an only child.'

'No,' she corrected, 'I told Charlotte I didn't have a brother or sister to look out for me.'

His expression went hard. 'That's semantics.'

She knew what he must be thinking—she'd lied to him, just as much as Camilla had. 'Ed, it's complicated. My family's not like yours. And you have no idea how much I envy you having George and the girls. They love you. I've never had that.' Her eyes pleaded for him to understand. 'The thing is, Jenna's like Mum. She's a super-model. And she takes after Mum emotionally as well as physically. She's fragile. Any cold or virus, she always gets it. She had glandular fever the other year, and couldn't work for six months. Whereas I've got the constitution of an ox and I'm almost never ill.' She sighed. 'I tried to look after her. When we were kids and Mum was ill, I'd cook dinner for us. Jenna can't so much as boil an egg. But she told me at the weekend that she's always hated me for it. She called me Little Dr Perfect.' She dragged in a breath. 'I thought I was being caring and kind and nurturing, looking after her, and she thought I was just showing off.'

Ed stood up and put his arms round her. 'Oh, honey. You're very far from being a show-off. If anything, you hide your light under a bushel.'

'She wanted to stay at my place on Saturday— she lives out of a suitcase most of the time, so she normally expects to stay with me if she's in London—but she was spoiling for a fight, the second she walked through the door. I shouldn't have risen to it, but…' Well, she wasn't going to blame Ed for the fact that she'd been worried about him. 'I just snapped. I told I was going out and I didn't want her there when I got back. She must've heard your message and worked every-thing out.' She swallowed hard. 'I haven't told her or my parents that I'm even seeing you and I'm so sorry. I never wanted you to get mixed up in all this. I'll understand if you don't want to see me again, and I'll write an apology to your family.'

'Jane, you don't have to do that. And no way

am I dumping you. It's not your fault that the story leaked.' He sighed. 'But I wish you'd told me about her before.'

'My relationship with my entire family is rubbish, and I'm not very good at being a failure. I guess she's right about me wanting to think I'm perfect.'

He stroked her hair. 'Nothing of the sort. It isn't you.'

'I'm the one who doesn't fit into my family. So it feels like it's me.'

'What does Sorcha say?' he asked.

She rolled her eyes. 'You don't want to know what she calls Jenna. Especially after...' She stopped.

'After what?'

Given that her sister had hurt his family like this, she owed him the truth. 'Shaun.'

He blinked. 'Your *twin* was the one you caught him with?'

'Yes. '

Ed shook his head, looking stunned. 'Wow. That's seriously... I'm not sure I could forgive George if he'd done that to me.'

'George would never do that to you. He loves you.' She shrugged. 'Jenna hates me.'

Ed looked her straight in the eye. 'Please tell me you weren't worrying that the same thing would happen with me? That I'd meet her and go off with her?'

'No, of course not. Jenna might have tried it on with you, but you're not Shaun. You have integrity. I know you would've turned her down if she'd come on to you. I didn't tell you about her because…because no matter what I do, I can't get close to her, and she makes me feel bad. And I hate that.'

'What a mess.' Ed leaned his forehead against hers. 'And I hate that you're feeling bad when none of it's your fault.'

'It is. Because if I hadn't blown up at Jenna and walked out, I would've been there to answer your call and she wouldn't have overheard the message. And she wouldn't have been mad at me for telling her to leave, and…' She shook her head. 'I need to talk to her and find out what the hell she was playing at. And then maybe I can call Dad and find out the number of Mum's old publicist, see if she can help with some damage limitation.'

'George is bound to know someone. So will Alice. Don't worry about it.'

Jenna wasn't answering her mobile, and her parents didn't answer their landline. Jane sighed. 'I'll try again later.'

'Janey. It's really not your fault.' Ed took her hand and kissed the back of her fingers. 'I know it wasn't you who leaked it. When I said to George I wanted to tell you, he said immediately that he trusted you, too.'

But, thanks to her family, she'd let him down. Broken their trust in her.

'You know, before all this blew up, I'd been thinking,' he said. 'You know I love you.'

'Even after this?'

'It's only talk. We can just ignore it. I'm sure worse things have been said about my family over the centuries.' He took a paperclip from his desk and began fiddling with it, then dropped to one knee in front of her. 'This is quite possibly the worst timing in the universe. I have no idea what the DNA results are going to show. If it's the wrong result, a lot of sticky stuff's going to hit the fan. All that "for richer, for poorer" stuff—I could be asking you to take an awful lot more of the rough than the smooth. And I know you've had a bad experience before, being engaged to someone who let you down badly. But I love you, Jane. I want to be with you, and life's a million times better with you than without you. And you're the one who's taught me I can put the past behind me and believe in the future. So will you do me the honour of marrying me, Jane?'

She caught her breath. 'Are you sure about this? I mean, with my mum and Jenna the way they are, it's never going to be easy with my family.'

He shrugged. 'They're difficult and they don't appreciate you. That's their problem. I'm not asking them to marry me—I'm asking you.' He reached up to stroke her face. 'For what it's worth, my family's got enough love to support us both through anything that happens in the future. But at the end of the day it's you and me. And I'll be right by your side, through the bad times as well as the good. So will you marry me, Jane?'

He was asking her to take a chance on him and

join her future with his. To risk having a lot more rough times than smooth times.

She'd been here before, full of hopes and listening to a speech that turned out to be a piecrust promise, empty and easily broken.

But Ed wasn't Shaun. He wasn't saying that life would be a perfect paradise and offering her the moon and the stars. He was offering her something better: something realistic and solid. A life that wasn't always going to be easy, but he'd always be by her side.

She bent down to kiss him. 'I'd be honoured. Yes.'

'Good.' He slid the makeshift ring onto the ring finger of her left hand and kissed her. 'Let's go shopping after work tonight and choose the real ring together.' He smiled. 'And it really doesn't matter if the paps follow us. It just means they'll have a nice story to print about my family instead of a pile of spite. And we're going to celebrate.'

CHAPTER FOURTEEN

JANE tried ringing Jenna's mobile and her parents' landline several times more before the end of her shift, and at last her father answered.

'Dad, is Jenna there?' she asked.

'Yes. She's in bed.'

Which meant that Jenna could be feeling guilty enough about what she'd done to push her into depression. Normally, Jane would be sympathetic about her twin's depression, but not after what she'd just done. This time, Jenna had gone way, way too far.

'I need to talk to her.'

'Is something wrong?'

You could say that again. But Jane also knew that Martin Cooper would go into protective father mode and make excuses for Jenna. He always did. And this time her twin had to face up to what she'd done. Jane made her voice sound as light as she could. 'I just need to talk to her about something, Dad.'

'She's resting. Can't it wait?'

'It's important.'

His voice hardened. 'She told me you threw her out.'

Jane sighed. Of course Jenna had got her story in first. And she wouldn't have said *why* Jane asked her to leave; she only ever told the bit of the story that made her look a victim. 'Dad, there are two sides to every story, OK? Please. I really need to talk to her.'

'To apologise?'

If that was what it took to get Jenna on the phone... 'Yes,' she fibbed.

Jenna took her time coming to the phone. 'What do you want?'

'The story in the press.'

'What story?'

'The one about Ed. I know you were the leak. You must've heard his message and worked it out for yourself.' Jane sighed. 'Look, I get that you hate me, but this time it isn't just me you hurt,

Jenna—you've hurt some really nice people, none of whom deserved this.'

'I was trying to help,' Jenna said defensively.

'Help? By spreading scandal in the tabloids? How do you work out *that's* helping?'

Jenna said nothing.

'You have to stop hurting people, Jenna. Or you're going to end up destroying yourself.'

Jenna's response was to hang up.

Two minutes later, Martin was on the phone to Jane. 'What the hell did you just say to her?' he demanded. 'She's breaking her heart down here.'

'Nothing like what I wanted to say, believe you me.' She put her father in the picture about exactly what Jenna had done, the people she'd hurt.

'It's a pity you don't think more about your *own* family,' Martin commented. 'You haven't even bothered seeing us this year.'

And they'd bothered coming to London to see her? Not. Jane finally saw red and everything she'd never said before came pouring out. 'Actually, Dad, have you ever considered things from *my* point of view? That Jenna expects and demands and takes all the time? And you let her get away with it. You never, ever tell her no. She can put the vilest stuff in the press about me, and it's fine, because it all boosts her career and that's far more important than not hurting me.'

'Jane! How can you say that?' He sounded shocked.

'Because it's true, Dad. You and Mum value looks above everything else. You've always made it clear that I'm the disappointment—the one who can't strut down a catwalk and be like Mum. But I'm doing just fine in my own field. You're the ones missing out. And in future you can just count me out. I'm tired of bending over backwards, being nice and saying nothing, no matter how badly Jenna behaves or how nasty she is.'

His silence gave her the courage to continue. 'And do you want to know why I've backed off from you all, why I haven't visited you this year? Then let me tell you why I gave Shaun his ring back last year. It's because I came home early and found him in bed with Jenna. My fiancé. In my bed. With my sister.'

'I had no idea.' He sounded stunned.

'Well, you do now. And this week she's leaked

that story to the press—a private message that was on my answering machine—and claimed she was trying to help. If you can work out how the hell hurting people she doesn't know—nice, genuine, kind people—is helping, then do let me know. Have a nice day.' Gritting her teeth, she replaced the receiver.

She'd well and truly burned her bridges, now, so she might as well make it complete. She sent her father an email with a link to the *Celebrity Life* interview. *When the journalist wanted to do the interview and photo shoot, I was doing my exams. I said I couldn't do it and explained why. This is the result. Perhaps now you'll understand why I've had enough. I just can't do this any more. And if you can't accept that, then perhaps I'm better off without all of you.*

She was brushing the tears away when Ed walked in. 'Janey? What's happened?'

She told him about her conversations with her father and Jenna. 'I think I've well and truly done it now. I've as good as given him an ultimatum.' She sighed. 'I guess it's been a long time coming.'

'Maybe it'll make a difference, now you've told them how you feel. Sometimes it takes a crisis and some hard words to make things work properly,' he said. 'Look at Pippa Duffield and her mother-in-law. You're the one who persuaded her to try building bridges, and her mother-in-law responded brilliantly.'

'I know, but I don't think this is going to work out for me,' Jane said.

He wrapped his arms round her. 'I'm so sorry, Janey. If it helps, you're most definitely part of my family, and they all love you to bits.' He kissed her. 'And we're going to make it official tonight.'

After work, Ed took Jane to choose the ring: a single diamond in a pretty platinum setting.

'Now you're officially mine,' he said, and kissed the back of her ring finger before sliding the diamond on to it. 'Do you mind if we call in to see George and share the good news?'

'No, I'd like that.'

Except when they got to George's flat, the whole of Ed's family was there; so were Sorcha and Jake, and champagne was chilling in the fridge.

'Ed? Did you organise all this, just this afternoon?' she asked.

'After you said yes?' He smiled. 'Yup. I thought we could all do with some good news to celebrate. Do you mind?'

'No—I'm just…' She swallowed hard. He'd done this to surprise her, to make her see that his family would drop everything at incredibly short notice to come and celebrate their engagement, because they considered her one of them.

He kissed the single tear away. 'I know. Your family should be here, too,' he said softly, guessing her thoughts accurately. 'That's why I asked Sorcha.'

Her best friend. 'The sister I wish I had.' And who would never, ever hurt her the way her biological sister had. 'Thank you.'

'I love you, and you love me. And whatever lies ahead, we're going to cope with it,' Ed said, holding her close. 'Together.'

* * *

The next morning, a huge hand-tied bouquet arrived for Jane at the hospital.

'How lovely. Your family works fast,' she said to Ed. Then she opened the card. 'Oh.'

'Who are they from?'

'Jenna.' Jane sat down. 'She's never apologised to me before. Ever.' She paused. 'Then again, they might not actually be from her.'

'How do you mean? Isn't her name on the card?'

'Dad likes a quiet life. I know the way his mind works.' She sighed. 'He thinks that if I believe Jenna's apologised, I'll let it go and things can carry on as they were.'

Ed looked surprised. 'You think your father sent them?'

She nodded. 'With the best of intentions. But it somehow makes everything feel worse.' She put the card back in the envelope and left it on her desk next to the flowers. 'We have rounds to do.'

'OK.'

It was a busy morning on the ward; halfway through their rounds, Rosie called them to come and look at a mum whose labour wasn't progressing.

'Why it's taking so long is that the baby's turned round and his back is against yours,' Jane explained.

'You've done a wonderful job, but you've been in labour all yesterday afternoon and all last night, you're tired now, and the baby's starting to get a little bit distressed. I think it's time to say enough,' Ed said gently. 'I'd recommend a section.'

'I'd so wanted a natural birth,' the mum said, looking miserable. 'I was going to do this with just gas and air. But I might as well make my birth plan into a paper plane.'

Ed squeezed her hand. 'Babies don't read birth plans. They have their own ideas,' he said with a smile. 'Come on. You've done brilliantly. If you really want to keep going for another half an hour, then I'll go with that, but if you haven't progressed any further then it's time to call it a day, for the baby's sake. Then we'll ask you to sign the consent form for a section.'

She sighed. 'It's not going to work, is it?'

Jane squeezed her other hand. 'I'm sorry, I don't think it will.'

'OK. I'll sign the form now.'

Half an hour later, she was cuddling her baby, and Jane was wiping away her usual tears of joy at helping a new life enter the world. She went to her desk to write up her notes, and realised that there was a registered post envelope on her desk. And she recognised the handwriting: Jenna's.

Warily, she opened the envelope.

Jane,

I'm sorry. I've always been jealous of you— you're the clever one, the strong one, and I'm as flaky and hopeless as Mum. You always make me feel as if I'm not good enough.

Jane stared at the words, barely taking them in. She'd made Jenna feel useless? But—that wasn't at all what she'd intended. She'd tried to make Jenna feel cherished, looked after.

I'm sorry I gave you a hard time when we were growing up. And I'm sorry for what I did to Ed and his family. I hope he doesn't dump you because of me. I'll apologise to him in person, if you want me to.

Jenna was actually apologising. Sincerely.

I hope you like the flowers. I sent them, not Dad.

So Jenna, too, knew how their father's mind worked.

I've had time to think about it. I know it's a lot to ask and I haven't been good to you, but can we start again? This time, as equals? Love, Jenna.

Ed came over. 'Janey, are you OK?'
Wordlessly, she handed him the card.
He read it swiftly. 'Wow. I would never have expected that.'
'Me neither. I don't…' She shook her head. 'I don't know what to think, how to react. I mean, it's the first time she's ever offered me any kind of olive branch.'

And then Gwen, one of the junior nurses, came over with another huge bouquet of flowers. 'Janey, is there something you're not telling us? Like it's your birthday or something?'

Jane exchanged a glance with Ed. There was something they weren't telling, yet, but they were waiting until the DNA results came back before they told the rest of the world. 'No, it's not my birthday. I had a fight with my sister.'

Gwen rolled her eyes. 'Tell me about it. I have those all the time—my sister never sends me flowers, though.'

'This is a first for her,' Jane said dryly. She opened the card and read it.

I'm sorry. Jenna's fragile, like your mother. You're like me, the one who gets on with things. I never meant you to feel second-best. You're not, and it won't happen again. I'm so proud of you, Jane. And I love you.
Dad.

'They're from my dad,' she said.
'Did you have a fight with him, too?' Gwen

looked surprised. 'You've never fallen out with anyone since I've known you. And then you had two fights in one night?'

Jane gave her a wry smile. 'I guess it's a bit like buses. You wait for ages, then two come along at once.'

'Well, they're lovely flowers,' Gwen said with a smile. 'Enjoy them, you lucky thing.'

When Gwen left, Jane handed the card to Ed.

'Judging by that card and all those flowers,' he said when he'd finished reading it, 'I think your family's finally started to see you for who you are—and realised your worth.'

'Maybe.' There was a huge lump in her throat. 'I'd better ring them. I have some making up to do.'

'Go for it. And come and grab me if you need me,' he said, and kissed her.

CHAPTER FIFTEEN

THE results of the test were due back on the Monday. Jane and Ed had both managed to swap shifts so they had a day off to wait in for the post; David and Frances had come up from Suffolk to stay with George; and the girls were all on standby to come straight over to Ed's flat as soon as the post arrived and he called them.

Ed couldn't settle to anything and was pacing the flat. There were lines of tension on his face, and he glanced at the clock every couple of seconds and then looked shocked that so little time had passed since he'd last looked.

'Oh, honey.' Jane kissed him lightly. 'There's not much longer to wait.' If only she could take this strain from him.

'This is worse than waiting for exam results to come. George said the same thing. You've always got a good idea how you did in your exams.

This…this is completely out of my control.' He shook his head in obvious frustration. 'I know who I am right now, but that envelope could tell me I'm someone completely different.'

Jane squeezed his hand. 'Ed, whatever the results are, you know they won't change how I feel about you. I love you for who you are, not for who your biological father is. And David will always, always see you as his son, regardless of what the test says.'

'I know. And thank you. Sorry. I'm being difficult.' He sighed. 'This waiting is killing me. I can't *breathe*, Jane. My chest feels tight and my head hurts, and it feels as if someone swapped my blood for ice.'

There was nothing she could say, nothing she could do, to make things better. Only hold him.

When the intercom buzzed, he froze. 'Oh, my God—the results are coming by registered post. That must be the postman now.' He rushed over to the intercom. 'Yes?'

'Can you *please* let us in before I start threatening the paps with my crutches and Alice has to bail me out in court?' George asked plaintively.

Ed buzzed him up and went to open his front door. Jane switched the kettle on and busied herself making coffee.

'The results aren't here yet,' she could hear Ed say. 'I said I'd call you the minute they came.'

'I just couldn't stand the wait any longer.'

'Even when they do turn up, you know we can't open them until the girls are here,' Ed warned. 'We promised.'

'True, but I'd still rather wait here with you.' George limped into the kitchen and hugged Jane. 'Hello, Janey. How's my favourite sister-in-law-to-be?'

'As nervous as you lot are,' she said. 'Ed can't settle to anything.'

'Me neither. I'm not good at waiting at the best of times, and this is driving me crazy,' George said.

'Especially as he had to put up with me driving us here from his flat,' David said wryly as he walked into the kitchen. 'Trust me, we're all desperate for his leg to be good enough for him to drive himself again, so we don't have to put up with all the instructions and comments.'

Frances ruffled George's hair. 'Don't listen to your dad, love. He's a worse passenger than you are—which is why I never drive him anywhere!'

Jane handed round mugs of coffee. Although she'd put cookies on a plate, nobody was hungry and they just sat there in the middle of the table.

'I wish there was a way you could just wind time forward,' George said.

'Me, too,' Ed agreed.

'We need to talk about something else. *Anything* else,' David said.

'The wedding?' George suggested. 'We can plan it all now. I mean, we have the bride here, the groom, the best man...'

'Do you seriously think we'd let you loose on the planning?' Jane asked. 'You'd have us getting married in mid-air on one of your paragliding things!'

'What a great idea, Janey.' George dimpled at her. 'Maybe we could offer that as one of the wedding packages in Suffolk.' Then he frowned. 'Well. Maybe not. It might not be my place to suggest that any more.'

'Of course it will be.' David rolled his eyes. 'I

already told you. I don't give a damn what the genetic specialists say; you're both my sons.'

'And mine,' Frances added. 'You don't have to be biologically related to be someone's parent.'

'Frances, you've been a much better mother to us than ours could ever have been,' Ed said quietly. 'Actually, George and I have thought of you as our mum for years.'

Jane could see Frances' eyes mist over with tears. 'Oh, Ed.'

'It's true,' George said. 'And, Dad—we couldn't have asked for anyone better than you.'

'I couldn't have asked for better sons. Even though you give me grey hairs with those damned extreme sports, George.' David patted his shoulder. 'Ed, how does this DNA thing work exactly?'

'They look at genetic markers. With every pair of genes, you inherit one from each parent. Obviously we couldn't give the lab a maternal sample, but if your DNA profile matches one of each pair of alleles in our DNA profile, then it proves you're our father.'

David was white-faced as he asked, 'And if it doesn't match?'

Ed took a deep breath. 'Then the results will say that they exclude you from the possibility of being our father.'

The minutes ticked by, slower and slower; none of them felt like making small talk, and the kitchen was filled with a silence so heavy that it weighed down on all of them. Ed resumed pacing, George drummed his fingers on his crutches, and David turned his cup round and round in his hands.

Finally, the intercom went again; this time, it really was the postman.

Ed buzzed him up, then said, 'George, ring the girls while I sign for the letters.'

When he came back, George said, 'They're all getting taxis. They'll be here in twenty minutes, tops.' He blew out a breath. '*Twenty more minutes*. Do we really have to wait for them?'

'Yes, we do—this is a family thing, and we're all in it together. Right, Jane?' Frances said.

It warmed Jane that Frances had included her. 'Right,' she agreed.

Finally the girls arrived; they all refused coffee and just leaned against the worktops in the kitchen, looking grim.

'OK. This is it,' Ed said, and swallowed hard. He ripped the first envelope open and unfolded the sheets of paper.

'And?' George asked impatiently.

Ed scanned the paper. 'Yours and Dad's markers match—it says there's a 99.9 per cent probability that Dad's your father. Which is as good as it gets.' He looked up and met his brother's gaze. 'Thank God.'

'And you?' David asked.

Ed took a deep breath and opened the other envelope. He looked at the sheet swiftly, and sagged in apparent relief. 'Me, too.'

'So all that stuff in her diaries and those letters... She was completely wrong,' George said.

'Your mother was completely wrong about an awful lot of things,' David said. 'I'm sorry that you both had to go through this.' He hugged both his sons. 'And now we tell the press the truth, and they'll can go and find someone else to write their stories about.'

'If this is an official statement, Dad, do you need it written down?' Alice asked.

'It'll be short and sweet,' David said. 'And, no,

I don't need to write it down. What I'm saying comes straight from the heart.'

The whole family, united, went down to the entrance to the flats. David stood between his sons. Flashes started popping, and there was a barrage of questions until it became very obvious that David had something to say and he wasn't going to answer a single question until they'd given him a chance to speak.

Eventually the hubbub died down.

'Thank you,' David said. 'I'm aware that you've all been interested in the paternity of my sons, George and Edward. So I'm delighted to announce that the DNA testing has conclusively...' His voice cracked, and he stopped.

George put his hand on his father's shoulder to bolster him.

'Conclusively proved that my sons are...' David stopped again.

Clearly their father had been bottling up his feelings all week. Despite his assertion that he hadn't needed to write anything down, emotion had robbed David of his voice and he couldn't make the announcement.

George widened his eyes at Ed and gave the tiniest nod.

Ed decoded the message: *you're the scientist—it's better coming from you.*

He lifted his chin. 'The DNA testing proves without a shadow of a doubt that George and I are our father's biological sons.'

There was murmuring from the press pack. Obviously this was robbing them of the scandal story they'd been hoping for.

Maybe it was time to give them something else instead. Something much, much more positive. He held out his hand to Jane.

She gave him a tiny nod, and stepped forward to take his hand.

'We also have some other news,' Ed said. 'I've found the love of my life and she's agreed to marry me. I know she'll mean every word of those vows, because she agreed to marry me before we knew the results of the testing, and she didn't care whether they'd make me a prince or a pauper. Dr Jane Cooper and I are going to get married as soon as possible.'

'So is there a third bit of news, Ed?' one of the journalists called out.

Ed laughed. 'You mean, are we getting married because we have to?' But this would be nothing like his marriage to Camilla. 'No.'

'We're getting married quickly,' Jane said, 'simply because we don't want to have to wait for the rest of our lives to start.'

'Exactly.' Ed pulled her into his arms, bent her back over one arm and kissed her. Thoroughly. And the flashing lightbulbs felt like stars exploding in his head.

The headlines the next morning ran, *George is the boy*.

And Jane smiled at the caption beneath the photograph of Ed kissing her speechless: *Ed with Dr Cinderella*.

The following Sunday afternoon, she and Ed headed down to Suffolk, with Sorcha and Jake following them; Alice had the task of driving George, and had threatened to ask Bea to bring gaffer tape to shut him up if he said a word out of place.

'We could've had a big party, you know,' Ed said. 'A marquee, a band, a chocolate fountain and lots of champagne.'

'I just wanted the important people there,' she said softly. 'A small, intimate family lunch to celebrate our engagement.'

Ed reached over to squeeze her hand. 'I spoke to your dad on Friday night. If they don't come, *don't* take it personally. It's at least a seven-hour drive from Cornwall to Suffolk, and that's assuming they don't get stuck in traffic.'

Which meant that they would've needed to drive up the day before and stay nearby. Jane was pretty sure that Frances would've offered to put the Coopers up, but she was equally sure that her mother would've refused the invitation.

Her father and Jenna had wished them well. Jenna had even said the photos in the press of Ed kissing Jane were gorgeous, like a fairy-tale. But there had been a resounding silence from Sophia.

Well, OK. Maybe her mother would thaw out by the wedding, next month.

Though Jane wasn't going to hold out much hope.

When they finally arrived at the hall, Frances greeted them warmly. 'Come through to the rose garden. David's spent all morning putting a gazebo up.' She glanced up at the skies. 'And it looks as if the weather's going to be kind, so we won't have to make a run for the house.'

George and the girls were already there, Sorcha and Jake were only a couple of minutes behind, and Jane was very, very aware of the empty places that would be at the end of the beautifully laid table. Where her family should've been.

'I thought a cold buffet might be best,' Frances said. 'Though I have hot new potatoes in the Aga, and the bread's still warm.'

Jane's eyes widened as she saw the spread. 'Wow. That's fabulous. Frances, you've gone to so much trouble. That's an awful lot of work.'

'It was a labour of love,' Frances assured her. 'We're so pleased you're going to be part of our family.'

If only her own family felt the same way. But she damped down the disappointment and forced herself to smile.

It was only when Ed nudged her and said softly,

'More guests to greet,' that she turned round and saw her parents walking across the lawn towards them, along with Jenna.

'Jane.' Sophia, as always, greeted her daughter with an air kiss. Jane tried very hard not to mind.

But Jenna surprised her with a warm hug. 'You look beautiful,' she said. 'My little sister.'

Jane blinked the tears back. 'Only by five minutes.'

And Martin surprised her further by holding her really, really tightly. 'Janey. My clever, special girl,' he whispered. 'I think your mother and I have got a lot of making-up to do to you.'

She swallowed hard. 'It doesn't matter, Dad. Not any more.'

'No, because you and Ed have each other. This one's going to do right by you.' He smiled at her. 'I never liked the other one in any case. He wasn't right for you. But Ed…he's the one.'

'He certainly is.'

She caught Ed's eye, and he mouthed, 'I love you.'

David tapped a wine glass with a fork. 'Now we're all here, I think we should have the official business before lunch.'

'Absolutely.' Ed took Jane's hand and led her to the middle of the gazebo. 'We already know Jane agreed to marry me when everything was going wrong and it looked as if she was going to have a lot more of the rough than the smooth. But that's all behind us now, and I think it's made all of us stronger. So today I want to do this properly and get engaged officially, with the people we love most in the world around us, and in a place that's special to both of us.' He dropped to one knee and opened the velvet-covered box, just as he'd done in her kitchen. 'Jane Cooper, I love you with my whole heart. Will you do me the honour of being my wife?'

There was only one answer she could possibly give. 'I love you, too. Yes.'

And as Ed slid the ring back on her finger, everyone cheered and George opened the champagne with a very, very loud pop.

AD

* * * * *

Mills & Boon® Large Print
Medical

October

GEORGIE'S BIG GREEK WEDDING?	Emily Forbes
THE NURSE'S NOT-SO-SECRET SCANDAL	Wendy S. Marcus
DR RIGHT ALL ALONG	Joanna Neil
SUMMER WITH A FRENCH SURGEON	Margaret Barker
SYDNEY HARBOUR HOSPITAL: TOM'S REDEMPTION	Fiona Lowe
DOCTOR ON HER DOORSTEP	Annie Claydon

November

SYDNEY HARBOUR HOSPITAL: LEXI'S SECRET	Melanie Milburne
WEST WING TO MATERNITY WING!	Scarlet Wilson
DIAMOND RING FOR THE ICE QUEEN	Lucy Clark
NO.1 DAD IN TEXAS	Dianne Drake
THE DANGERS OF DATING YOUR BOSS	Sue MacKay
THE DOCTOR, HIS DAUGHTER AND ME	Leonie Knight

December

SYDNEY HARBOUR HOSPITAL: BELLA'S WISHLIST	Emily Forbes
DOCTOR'S MILE-HIGH FLING	Tina Beckett
HERS FOR ONE NIGHT ONLY?	Carol Marinelli
UNLOCKING THE SURGEON'S HEART	Jessica Matthews
MARRIAGE MIRACLE IN SWALLOWBROOK	Abigail Gordon
CELEBRITY IN BRAXTON FALLS	Judy Campbell

Mills & Boon® Large Print Medical

January

SYDNEY HARBOUR HOSPITAL: MARCO'S TEMPTATION	Fiona McArthur
WAKING UP WITH HIS RUNAWAY BRIDE	Louisa George
THE LEGENDARY PLAYBOY SURGEON	Alison Roberts
FALLING FOR HER IMPOSSIBLE BOSS	Alison Roberts
LETTING GO WITH DR RODRIGUEZ	Fiona Lowe
DR TALL, DARK...AND DANGEROUS?	Lynne Marshall

February

SYDNEY HARBOUR HOSPITAL: AVA'S RE-AWAKENING	Carol Marinelli
HOW TO MEND A BROKEN HEART	Amy Andrews
FALLING FOR DR FEARLESS	Lucy Clark
THE NURSE HE SHOULDN'T NOTICE	Susan Carlisle
EVERY BOY'S DREAM DAD	Sue MacKay
RETURN OF THE REBEL SURGEON	Connie Cox

March

HER MOTHERHOOD WISH	Anne Fraser
A BOND BETWEEN STRANGERS	Scarlet Wilson
ONCE A PLAYBOY...	Kate Hardy
CHALLENGING THE NURSE'S RULES	Janice Lynn
THE SHEIKH AND THE SURROGATE MUM	Meredith Webber
TAMED BY HER BROODING BOSS	Joanna Neil